Gideon

A Walker Brothers Novel

Seven Sons Ranch in Three Rivers Romance™
Book 8

Liz Isaacson

ISBN-13: 978-1-63876-369-7

1

Gideon Walker left the farmhouse where he'd grown up and headed for the detached garage. "Come on, you lazy things," he said to the two dogs lying in the shade beneath the porch. "Let's go to the park."

Mack got up, a goofy grin perpetually on his face. He was a big, black animal with absolutely no sense whatsoever. But as he trotted alongside Gideon, a sweet sense of camaraderie moved through the man. He barked at something only he could see or smell, and Gideon ducked inside the garage to get their leashes.

"Hey, Daddy," he said when he found his father inside, working on the riding lawn mower. His dad twisted the wrench, trying to get the bolt to move. It didn't.

"Hey, son." He sighed and looked over to Gideon. The atmosphere changed, though Gideon tried to ignore it. He reached for the leashes, but both dogs had wandered off, probably in search of a squirrel or prairie dog. Mack especially had the attention span of a gnat, and Gideon had chased him down at the park just yesterday to get him to stay away from a family of geese.

"Goin' to the park?"

"Yeah," Gideon said. "What's going on with that?"

"Oh, it keeps stalling." Daddy looked over to Gideon. "You're really going back to Austin in the fall?"

Gideon sighed and looked away. "Yes, Daddy." It was July, and Gideon had finally told his parents he wanted to return to the university in Austin in the fall instead of staying to work the family ranch. He loved it here, under the shade of all the trees, the still air—especially at night— that allowed a man to truly think, and the scent of horses and freshly mown hay.

He'd worked hard growing up, and he didn't mind it. But the fact was, Gideon was the middle son. He'd never expected to inherit the ranch, and he'd only just realized that his father had wanted him to go to college, and then, Gideon was expected to come home and work the ranch. That was just what Walkers did.

Gideon didn't want to be that brand of Walker.

His father returned to the lawn mower, and Gideon wondered if it really wasn't running. His father loved to tinker with mechanical things, and Gideon didn't hate it either.

He whistled for Mack and Moose, because he was tired of this same old conversation. Mack came trotting over, and Gideon held up his fist, the universal sign to get the dog to sit. Mack just stood there, panting, and Gideon rolled his eyes as he clipped the leash to the dog's collar.

He looked around for Moose, but the other dog had disappeared.

"I think you and Jonas and Spencer can work the ranch together," Daddy said. "That's what we've always planned for."

Gideon usually enjoyed the personal connection he and his daddy had, and all of his best memories had originated in this garage while they fiddled with something, or organized lumber for a new construction project, or held their ranch meetings. Only Jonas and Daddy met about the ranch now, though, and Gideon hadn't even been told the truth.

He didn't want to hurt his father, but he'd never been completely honest with him about why he wanted to go back to Austin this fall. He'd never revealed what he knew.

"I don't want the ranch," Gideon said.

"What are you going to do then?"

"I already told you, Daddy. I want to go back to school."

"You graduated."

Gideon drew in a deep breath through his nose. "I know. I got a degree in business. I could buy my own ranch, or help run this one right. But I don't want to." He wanted to explore so much more of the world than Sweet Creek in the Texas Hill Country. The world was wide open right now, and the possibilities felt absolutely endless to Gideon.

"What are you going to do?" his dad asked again.

"Well." Gideon tried to choose his words carefully. His father got overwhelmed easily, especially with new things—the very things that brought excitement to Gideon's soul. "You've heard of the microwave oven. Someone invented that. And I was reading an article the other day about fiber optics, Daddy. They can send pulses of light through a *fiber*."

"A fiber?"

And Gideon had lost him. "There are people working on so many things," he continued anyway. "The space program uses computers, and they're getting smaller and smaller." He started speaking faster, trying to get his point across before his father started shaking his head and waving his hand, a signal that he was done listening.

"People *invent* those things, Daddy. I want to learn the technology. *I* want to invent the things people will use in the future." The need to do so practically seethed beneath his skin, making standing still difficult and uncomfortable.

Gideon didn't want to stand still. He wanted to get out there in the world and *do* something.

"So you're going to go work at NASA?"

"Maybe," Gideon said. "But not right away. I need to take more classes."

"You've just spent the last four years in classes."

Gideon sighed, because this was a losing conversation. He wished things could be different, but the fact was, they couldn't.

"I know you had Jonas sign the documents to make the ranch his."

That got Daddy to stop tinkering with the blasted lawn mower. His eyes met Gideon's, and he saw so much of himself in the dark depths.

Everything about the Walker men existed in shades of darkness. Dark hair, and Daddy's was some of the darkest. Gideon's was lighter, though not by much.

Dark brown eyes, and again, Daddy had the deepest, darkest pair. Gideon's rivaled his though, especially when he was frustrated or angry.

He tanned easily, and he seemed to be able to eat whatever he wanted and still stay trim. His height contributed to that, and the fact that he'd once loved to lift his father's barbells, which he kept in the barn, before he left for school each day.

Moose came bounding toward the garage, and Gideon masked his frustrated sigh as a grunt as he bent to clip the second leash onto the dog's collar. Moose was a big, hairy, brown dog who was named after the animal he most represented. The mutt had long legs that didn't seem to move the right way, so he always seemed one step away from falling completely.

He had a big snout too, and he loved to run around the park and sniff everything—and everyone—he could. Most people around Sweet Creek knew Moose, because while he was big and clumsy, he at least had some intelligence.

There wasn't a dog kennel in the county that could hold Moose, and not just because of his size. Gideon swore the dog's paws morphed into human hands when he was alone, because he could open doors.

"Come on," he said to the two dogs. "Load up. We're going to the park."

His father watched him, still silent and not admitting that he'd passed the ranch to Jonas, which everyone knew left nothing for Gideon or Spencer.

"Momma's got dinner on," his dad said as Gideon got behind the wheel.

"I won't be late," Gideon promised, and he got off the ranch as quickly as he could without spitting gravel behind his tires. He wanted to, but he knew from experience that his show of anger would only land him in hotter water with Daddy.

"Work the ranch together," Gideon scoffed. "There's no *together* if Jonas owns the whole thing, Daddy."

He continued to rant as he drove to town. Sweet Creek wasn't a huge place in the Hill Country, but it had a decent number of people in town and the surrounding hills. Probably ten thousand or so.

Their department stores had the microwave ovens Gideon had spoken of, though his momma hadn't purchased one. When they'd first been introduced, Fisher's had put one in the front display window and done hourly demonstrations.

Gideon remembered them clearly, and perhaps that had been when the invention bug had bitten him. "No," he told himself. "You've always wanted to push the boundaries. Explore the new. Make something out of nothing." And that was true.

Gideon Walker had the drive and intelligence to invent, and he wouldn't settle for working a ranch he didn't own and had no chance of owning.

"There's no future for me here." He wanted to be somewhere important, somewhere where things happened, where men thought outside of boxes, and where fences didn't exist.

He pulled up to the sprawling park across the street from the church he'd attended for the first eighteen years of his life. For a moment, relief pulled through him.

After he threw the ball for Moose and managed to tucker out Mack, perhaps he could go sit down on one of the benches and pray for guidance.

The wind picked up, and Gideon pressed his hand down on his cowboy hat so it wouldn't get stolen. Heaven knew he'd lost plenty of hats to a stiff breeze, especially around these parts of Texas.

"Come on," he said to the dogs. "Now stay by me,

okay? There are a lot of people here today." Summer in Texas usually took people to the water parks, the rivers, the lakes. This park had a lake in the middle of it, and plenty of grass surrounding that. Enormous cypress trees kept things shaded, and families brought blankets and picnic baskets to spend afternoons together. Couples snuck off to the more private parts of the park, and Gideon had seen black rabbits in the park year-round.

Mack especially liked to chase them, and Gideon swept the patch of park he'd chosen for the dogs. It was remote enough, hopefully, to keep them entertained, but out of other people's hair. Mack didn't have personal boundaries, and he thought everyone he met had just come to give him a pat.

Moose didn't know his own strength, that was all. They were both kind, gentle dogs. They just required the right kind of person to love them.

Gideon did love them, but not as much as Daddy. Daddy had always loved dogs, and they had at least fifteen on the ranch. Maybe more. Momma had put her foot down when the third dog had started coming inside to sleep and eat, and Daddy got more dogs as a way to "rescue them."

"Stay by me," he told the dogs again, and he picked up the ball Moose loved to chase. He threw it as far as he could and reached for the bowl he'd fill with water from the drinking fountain.

No beast—man or canine—could go long in the July

Texas heat without a good, long, cold drink of water. Gideon's mouth felt dry right that instant, in fact.

He watched Moose and Mack chase after the ball. Moose got it, of course. Mack didn't even seem to know there was a ball present, but he loved to run alongside his friend.

"Bring it," Gideon called, but Moose just dropped the ball and trotted over to a tree, his sniffer working overtime.

Irritation flared in Gideon's soul. "Just bring it back," he muttered as he started across the lawn toward the pair of dogs.

He kept his eyes on them, because they could bolt at a moment's notice. Thankfully, they didn't, and he picked up the ball and threw it again.

Both dogs took off after it, and once again, Moose retrieved it, but didn't bring it back.

"Come on," he called. "Bring it." He should've brought some jerky or liver with him, but he'd been too frustrated by his conversation with his father to think of it.

Moose lifted his head suddenly, and Gideon yelled his name. But the dog wouldn't be deterred, and he took off at a sprint.

"No!" Gideon called. "Moose, come back. Come back!" He broke into a jog too, though his cowboy boots weren't really made for running on grass.

Various trees made it hard to see what had sparked Moose's attention. A squeal filled the air, followed by a hearty, feminine laugh, and Gideon rounded a tree to find both of his dogs, tails wagging, standing over a woman on the ground.

"Guys," he said, his heartbeat the thing that was sprinting now. "Come on. Leave her alone." He ran toward her, saying, "I'm sorry. Sorry. Moose. Mack. Come on."

But both dogs had gone deaf, and Gideon wanted to march them right over to the truck and lecture them the whole way back to the ranch.

Back to the ranch.

Boy, he didn't want to go back there.

"Sorry." He reached the blanket where the woman had been sitting and managed to wrestle Moose away from her. His long tongue still tried to lick her face while Gideon reached for Mack.

"Go on now. Sit down. Stay." Miraculously, the dogs did what he said, and Gideon turned his attention to the woman with the splay of dark auburn hair across her face.

She giggled like getting attacked by two seventy-pound dogs was the highlight of her day. And then she sat up, brushing her hair off her face.

Gideon froze at the sight of the most beautiful woman he'd ever met. Along with the auburn hair, she had smooth, tan skin, straight, white teeth, and the loveliest pair of green eyes he'd ever seen.

"It's fine," she drawled, grinning at him. "I love dogs."

He extended his hand toward her, the motion he'd

been about to make before she'd made his heart start to beat in a strange way.

She put her hand in his, and he helped her to her feet.

She brushed a couple of leaves and plenty of grass from her pants, which flared at the ankle but hugged her thigh. She was slim, but what she lacked in physicality, she made up for in charisma.

She wore a mauve sweater that accentuated her curves, with a deep neckline that Gideon yanked his eyes away from. All he could do was return the smile that still sat on her face.

She seemed made of sunshine and charm, and Gideon wanted to know everything about her. "I'm Gideon Walker," he said, extending his hand toward her again. He'd been numb the last time her skin had touched his, but this time, he felt every spark of attraction moving through him.

"Penny."

"Short for something?" he asked, barely keeping an eye on the dogs. He only seemed to have eyes for her now.

"Penelope."

He nodded. "Do you live around here, Penny?"

"Yeah," she said, grinning as Mack ran toward her. She bent down and scratched behind his ears. "My family owns the egg farm south of town." She glanced up at him, and Gideon nearly lost himself in those eyes. That smile. "Aarons is my last name."

"Oh, right," he said. "The Aarons Egg Farm. I've been by there."

She straightened, and Gideon reached down deep inside himself for another round of courage. "Would you like to go to dinner with me?"

"Hey, Penny," a man said as he came around the tree. "They didn't have anything but water." He looked at Gideon and Mack and moved right to Penny's side. He handed her a bottle of water, which Penny took and twisted off the cap.

"Thanks, Lee." She smiled at him too, and Gideon's heart flopped like a fish out of water. She'd heard him ask her out. He couldn't take the words back.

"This is Gideon," she said to Lee before turning to Gideon. "And this is Lee."

"Nice to meet you," Gideon said, but he didn't think it was nice at all. Moose barked, and Gideon turned away in time to see the dog streak away. "Sorry again about the dogs." He strode away, never more grateful for the disobedient canines than he was in that moment.

He rounded them up and threw the ball a few more times, forcing himself not to even look to his right. Penny hadn't even seemed surprised when he'd asked her to dinner, but Gideon kept wondering where the words had come from.

He wasn't shy with women; he simply hadn't really met anyone he'd wanted to go out with for very long. Penny's laughing green eyes stuck with him long after he'd loaded up the dogs and driven back to the ranch. Maybe

Lee was just her brother. Maybe she would've said yes to his dinner invitation if they hadn't been interrupted.

"Aarons Egg Farm," he muttered to himself as he closed up the horse barn for the night. His family ranch sat north and west of town, with the egg farm south. He knew of the Aarons, but he didn't know much more about them.

He definitely wanted to learn more.

2

Penelope Aarons had just stepped back into the house after a morning of crating eggs when her brother Darren looked up from his bowl of cereal. Probably his third or fourth bowl. "There's a guy here for you," he said in a bored voice.

Penny looked toward the sitting room, which she couldn't actually see, because the door leading from the front of the house to the back of it was closed. Her mother taught piano lessons in the sitting room, which was immediately off the front entrance, and with that door closed, the rest of the family didn't have to listen to *Twinkle, Twinkle Little Star* on repeat.

"Is Momma teaching this morning?"

"She finished," Darren said, turning a page in the newspaper.

"Who is it?"

"I can't keep track of the boys who come asking for you, Pen," Darren said, glancing up. "He was wearing a cowboy hat."

"Thanks. That's *so* helpful," Penny said. But that one tidbit told her something—it wouldn't be Lee. Lee didn't stop by the house without making plans with her first anyway.

Penny stepped over to the kitchen sink and started washing her hands. Who had she met in the past few days that would go to the trouble of looking up where she lived, and then come by? Her heartbeat fluttered in her chest. The cowboy with the dogs. At the park.

Gideon Walker.

"Momma's chatting him up," Darren said. "You might want to hurry. He's been here at least ten minutes already."

"What did you tell him?" She couldn't entertain hope for the man to be Gideon. They'd barely talked, though he had asked her to dinner. Penny was used to being asked out, honestly. And she almost always went.

Darren wasn't lying when he said he couldn't keep track of the men who came around the house. Penny could barely keep track of them.

"I said you were working, but you should be done in a few minutes. He said he'd wait." Darren turned another page, clearly not reading anything in the paper. "Momma finished her lesson, and now they're talking."

"Okay." Penny dried her hands and took a big breath, her slight shoulders lifting and falling quickly.

"It's just another guy, Pen," Darren said without looking at her. "You'll laugh with him, and have him buy you dinner, and then you'll tell him you're leaving for Austin in a month, and that will be that."

"Yeah, probably," Penny said. She needed to have that conversation with Lee too. She liked him, but he had no ambition. No drive. No vision beyond Sweet Creek and what he already had here.

Penny wanted *more*. She didn't care that she was the only female student in the pre-law program at UT-Austin. She could handle the snide remarks and sexist comments from her male counterparts. All she had to do was study harder than them, score higher than them.

They'd take her seriously one day.

She walked past her brother at the dining room table and turned toward the front door. She opened the closed door separating her and the sitting room and paused as her mom laughed lightly.

"I'll go check on her," she said, and Penny stepped into the room and came face-to-face with her mother. "Oh, here she is." Momma's eyes held sparkle and hope as she widened them, mouthing *He's great.*

Penny nodded and looked past her mother to see who'd come by. Sure enough, Gideon Walker stood there, and Penny suddenly felt like she should've done more than just wash her hands. She should've showered, *and* blown out her hair, *and* put on makeup and perfume, *and* changed out of her stinky egg-crating clothes.

"Hey," Gideon said, taking a step forward.

Penny heard the soft click of the door behind her as her mother left the room. He scanned her from head to toe, a smile forming on that strong mouth. It fit solidly on his face, which bore a square jaw with plenty of sexy stubble that was nearly black.

Tall. Dark. Handsome. He had it all.

"Hello." Penny reached up and self-consciously tucked her hair, her gaze dropping to Gideon's hands, which went round and round each other. So he was nervous too.

Penny wasn't even sure what to do with her nerves. She wasn't used to having them when it came to men. She knew she was beautiful, because everyone told her she was. She'd developed early, and she'd had boys calling the house and waiting along the fence where she walked from the egg warehouse to her house to talk to her in the morning before junior high school.

"Your mother says you crate the eggs in the morning," he said, reaching up to adjust that delectable cowboy hat.

Penny had grown up and graduated from high school in Texas, and she sure did like cowboys. Gideon had all the right pieces too—the hat, the boots, the jeans with barely a flare.

This morning, Penny wore a blue pair of shorts, as the warehouse didn't have air conditioning in the packing area, and a bright blue blouse that likely had smeared egg yolk on it.

"Yeah, working, among other things," she said. "But today was crating. Mm hm." She put a smile on her face, hoping it would calm them both. "What brings you by?"

Gideon looked like he might throw up, and his anxiety actually helped her settle further. "I was hoping you'd tell me that guy you were with at the park the other day was your brother." He nodded toward the door behind her. "Then I met your brother, and I know he wasn't." He exhaled and removed his cowboy hat with one hand and ran his hand through his thick, dark hair with the other. "But I couldn't get myself to leave."

Penny indicated the chair her mom had likely been sitting in. She took it, and Gideon regained his seat too. "I know you heard me ask you to dinner, and I'm wondering what the possibility of that is."

Penny folded her hands in her lap and cocked her head at him. "I'm seeing Lee."

"Are you?"

Penny knew he'd seen her with him. She hadn't tried to hide her relationship with him in the park. Gideon had *seen* her. A sigh blew out of her mouth. "I mean, yes?"

"It sounds like you're not sure."

"Summer's almost over," she said.

"Oh, so it's a fling," Gideon said.

"No." Penny straightened her back, a fire roaring to life inside her. "I don't do flings."

"But you'll break up with him when you go back to school." Gideon watched her with a pair of dancing, dark eyes, the intensity in them calling to Penny. She felt the same intensity bubbling inside of her too, and she wondered if she'd finally met a man who could keep up with her.

Most of her boyfriends couldn't. Hadn't been able to. She hadn't been out with anyone for longer than four months, and her relationship with Lee was half of that.

And about to be over, she thought, as Gideon put his forearms on his knees and studied her.

"Yes," she finally said. "I'm planning to break up with him when I go back to Austin. Happy now?"

Gideon grinned. He even chuckled a little bit. "Not even slightly, Miss Penny. The only thing that would make me happy right now is you telling me we can go to dinner together."

"Persistent, aren't you?"

"When I know what I want."

"I'm not an object to be had," she said.

"Oh, I know that, ma'am." He stood up, that gorgeous smile making him twice as handsome. He wasn't nervous anymore either, and Penny liked that too. She wanted a man who would provide for her and protect her. Not someone to placate her, or cow tow to everything she said.

Gideon stepped toward the front door and opened it.

Pausing in the doorway, he turned back to her. "If you think you might could break up with Lee earlier, I'll be at The Capital tonight at seven. If you want to eat together, I'm sure I'll have an extra chair at my table." With that, he walked out, and Penny sat there stunned.

She jumped to her feet and hurried the few steps to the doorway, bracing herself against the doorjamb as she watched Gideon walk back to his truck.

The two big dogs that she'd met in the park stood in the back, both of them with their front paws up on the wheel well, smiling at her with their tongues hanging out.

Gideon glanced at her as he got behind the wheel, but he didn't smile or tip his hat.

Penny giggled to herself as he backed out of the driveway, her mind racing in several different directions. She stepped out of the doorway and closed the door, then went into the kitchen.

"Well?" Momma stood at the sink, her hands sudsy.

"Well, what?" Penny asked.

Momma rolled her eyes. "Don't be cute with me. He's so much more than anyone else you've been out with."

"That's because he's older than me."

"Praise the Lord," Momma said. "Aren't you tired of dating boys barely out of high school?"

Penny was, yes. She admitted it, which only fueled Momma's tongue. "Then you go out with Gideon. He's *very* nice, Pen. Articulate. Educated. Smart, that one. I could tell just by looking at him."

"Yeah," Penny said, because she'd been able to tell the same thing. "He wants me to go to dinner with him tonight at The Capital."

"Great," Momma said, though she literally loathed The Capital. She wouldn't go there anymore, because the last time she'd been, they'd charged her to switch the brown gravy for country gravy.

Penny shook her head, but she couldn't shake the smile in her soul. "I'm going to go read and shower," she said.

"Are you going to go to dinner with him?"

"I haven't decided yet," Penny said as she walked away.

She couldn't decide as she showered. She tried reading, but the book couldn't hold her attention. She had a few chores on the farm in the afternoon, and as she went down the rows of chickens to feed them, she considered going back to the house and getting ready to drive to town. She could take her mother's station wagon, as Momma had offered it to her when Penny went running out the back door to feed the chickens.

But, back at the house, she didn't start getting ready to go to dinner. She had a few hours anyway, and she sat down in front of the sewing machine in her bedroom. Penny loved to sew, and she'd learned from her grandmother when she was a little girl. She couldn't remember a time when the needle and thread, the fabrics and patterns hadn't soothed her.

Her mind whirred with the machine as she continued to work on a dress she'd been making for a couple of days. It would be ready for church on Sunday, and she had a vision of walking into the chapel wearing her new dress and scanning the congregation for Gideon Walker....

She sat back from the dress, having just finished a seam. She left it right where it was and glanced at the clock. Five-thirty. She had time to get ready and get to The Capital.

Her pulse skipped every third beat as she fixed her hair just right and applied makeup. She couldn't believe she was going to do this. She barely knew Gideon Walker.

"Momma," she called as she went racing down the steps. She turned toward the kitchen, saying, "Momma, I need the—" She cut off when she met her mother's eyes. Wide and round, she nodded past Penny to the sitting room while she dried her hands on a kitchen towel.

"What is it?" she asked.

"Lee's here," Daddy said, stepping over to her. He pressed a kiss to her forehead. "You sure look nice, sweetheart. Where's he taking you tonight?"

"I...don't know," Penny said. She didn't have plans with Lee that night. She stepped away from her father, her chest stinging as she walked into the sitting room. Lee was her boyfriend, though, and she definitely needed to fix her relationship status before she went romping off to The Capital to meet another man.

Sure enough, Lee sat in the sitting room—in the same chair Gideon had been in that morning—and he didn't even get up when she entered. "Lee," she said, seeing her romantic dinner with Gideon fade before her eyes. "What are you doing here?"

3

Gideon thanked the waitress as she set down a plate of bacon and cheese fries, the smile that came to his face only lasting for a blip in time. He couldn't help glancing toward the entrance to the restaurant as he picked up his napkin and put it on his lap.

Penny didn't walk in.

"She's not going to," he muttered to himself. Foolishness filled him from top to bottom, and it undulated through him in waves. He had no idea what had possessed him to show up at her house unannounced and act like he was the king of the world, inviting her to dinner with him when she had a boyfriend.

Not only that, but Gideon didn't meet women for dinner. He went to their house and picked them up, like a proper gentleman.

The bacon and cheese didn't even soothe him, and

when the waitress returned, she looked concerned. "Everything all right?" she drawled, looking at his nearly full plates.

"Yes," Gideon said, trying on that smile again. "Honestly, it's great. I'm just...not feeling well." He dropped his napkin on the table beside his steak sandwich. "Can you box it all up for me?"

"Sure thing." She took his food and Gideon got his money out in the few minutes it took for her to return. "Hope you feel better," she said.

"Thanks." Gideon's foul feelings had nothing to do with the food, but he took it all home anyway. He didn't go inside the homestead though, because then he'd have to explain himself. He hadn't told his parents he was meeting a woman for dinner, because he was twenty-two years old, and he didn't need their permission to drive the truck he owned to town and eat.

He sat on the front porch with Moose and Mack, his mind moving through his next steps. They changed every other second, though, and Gideon couldn't believe Penny Aarons hadn't shown up. He'd been so sure she would.

He could feel a snapping, crackling energy between them, but maybe she hadn't. She sure hadn't liked him calling her relationship with Lee a fling, but honestly, that was what it was.

"Yeah, and you're going back to Austin in a month too," he told himself. "So what are you doing?"

She said she'd go back to Austin too, his mind whispered at him. They'd be in the same city. He could definitely see her for longer than a month. New scenarios ran through his mind now, but in the end, Gideon dismissed them all. He wasn't going to go back to the Aarons Egg Farm again. Penny knew his intentions. He'd asked her out twice now. Shown up at her house unannounced and talked with her mother for a good fifteen minutes before Penny had come into the room.

He'd been bold and to the point, because he saw no reason to act otherwise. If she didn't like him, she didn't like him. He wasn't going to make a bigger fool of himself.

Sighing, he finally went inside the homestead when darkness began to cover the ranch. Thankfully, Momma had turned off the lights in the kitchen already, and Gideon didn't have to explain anything to anyone.

The next morning, Gideon woke early, as usual. He went out onto the ranch, the same as he'd done for many mornings over many years. He opened the horse barn and fed the horses, Mack and Moose never too far from him.

Jonas and Spencer and Daddy all worked around the ranch too, but Gideon kept his head down, the brim of his cowboy hat obscuring his face, and simply got the job done. When he left for Austin again, Jonas would hire on a new man, just as he'd done for the past four years.

There was nothing for him to feel guilty about. Jonas owned the ranch now. It was up to him to work it. He'd been dating a woman named Rosalee for several months now, but Gideon hadn't heard any talk of marriage or a wedding.

He finished with the horses and had just left the barn when Moose started barking. He and Mack ran toward the homestead and around the side of it at top speed, their voices so loud in the quietness of the ranch.

"What's that about?" Daddy asked as he came out of the calf shed.

"I'll go see," Gideon said. "It's probably just one of Momma's friends. Wasn't she doing that preserves exchange?"

"Mm," Daddy said, already distracted by something else.

Gideon followed the dogs around the house to find a brown station wagon parked in front of the homestead. A woman laughed at the dogs, and Gideon's feet froze to the ground and his chest seized up, making his heart work twice as hard to beat in the now-cramped space.

He knew that laugh, though he'd only heard it one other time.

Penny Aarons straightened and glanced toward the house. "Where is he, guys? Huh?"

He forced himself to keep walking, and her eyes came to his. The smile slipped from her face despite Moose's attempts to cheer her up. "Hey," she said, lifting her hand in a half-hearted wave. "I'm glad I found the right place."

"The arch gives us away," Gideon said. Everyone in Texas had a gate leading onto their property, and Daddy had erected an arch above the dirt lane that led back into these trees. The name WALKER had been carved into the wood in huge letters, and surely she hadn't wondered if she'd found the right ranch.

"Yes," she said. "It was a bit obvious." She turned and looked down the road she'd driven up. "I've just never been up this far, and I wasn't sure if I'd passed it or what."

He noticed a brown bag clutched in her hand. "What are you doing here?" he asked.

She brought her eyes back to his, and Gideon thought that was entirely unfair. She had to know what those big green eyes did to a man, and boy, did she know how to use them. Right now, they filled with regret and compassion, and Gideon wanted to assure her that everything was fine. He was fine.

Something nagged at him that said he wasn't.

She lifted the brown paper sack. "I brought breakfast."

"If that's not a cream cheese bear claw, you can get in the car and go," he teased.

Her whole countenance lit up, and Gideon couldn't help basking in the glow of it. Today, she wore a pink blouse covered in a flowery print and a pair of those flared jeans. She obviously kept up with the fashions of the day, and she seemed entirely out of his league.

"As a matter of fact," she said, opening the bag. "That's exactly what I brought."

He closed the distance to where she stood at the front of her car and peered inside the bag. A cream cheese bear claw sat there. He lifted his gaze to hers. "How did you know?"

"Lucky guess," she said.

"No one's that lucky." He indicated the porch steps and added, "Do you want to sit down for a minute?"

"Sure." They moved over to the steps and sat, both dogs following them like shadows. She took his bear claw out of the bag with a napkin and handed both to him. "I got myself a raspberry fritter."

"I like those too," he said. "But not as much as these." He took a big bite of the pastry, the sweet and creamy taste of it making his taste buds sing.

She smiled and took a much more delicate bite of her breakfast. She dusted off her hands and swallowed only a moment later. "I'm really sorry I didn't come last night."

Gideon's throat narrowed, but he took another enormous bite of the bear claw anyway. He didn't want to talk about last night.

"I wanted to," she said. "I was ready and everything, and then...Lee showed up."

Gideon nodded, his imagination conjuring up an image of the two of them dancing the night away. Penny definitely seemed like the type of woman to enjoy dancing, and Gideon wanted to hold her in his arms and experience her smile and laughter as they twirled together.

"I broke up with him," she said, nudging Gideon with her shoulder.

"You did?" He looked at her, surprise streaming through him.

"Yeah," Penny said, gazing out over the front yard. "You were right—I was going to break up with him anyway." She smiled and ducked her head. After she took another bite of her fritter, chewed, and swallowed, she added, "There's this other man I kinda wanted to go out with, too."

Hope exploded through Gideon, but he managed to tame his voice into normalcy when he asked, "Is that right?"

"Yeah, that's right."

"Lucky man," Gideon said, and that caused Penny to laugh. The light, carefree, feminine sound of it dove right into his ears, and he sure did like the sound of it. He chuckled too, and Penny linked her arm through his and let her forearm rest on his thigh.

"It's you, Gideon Walker, if you'll forgive me for standing you up last night."

He looked at her, but they were sitting so close, it almost made him go cross-eyed. He focused out in front of him again as Moose finally laid down. "I think I can do that," he said, his voice definitely a little gruff now.

"Good." Penny pressed her shoulder against Gideon's, and they sat on the front porch in silence while they finished their breakfast.

Gideon loved the peace this ranch had always provided for him, and after he'd brushed the crumbs from his hands, he asked, "So dinner tonight? I can come pick you up nice and proper this time."

"Yes," Penny said.

"Six-thirty?" he asked.

"That works." She stood, a sigh coming from her mouth. "I better get going. I told my momma I wouldn't be gone long, and she needs the car this afternoon."

"Okay." Gideon got to his feet too and walked with Penny toward the station wagon. "You're going to UT-Austin, right?" he asked.

"That's right," she said. "You?"

"I graduated in the spring," he said. "But I'm going back to take more classes. I'm hoping to get a job at one of the tech firms in the area. Texas Instruments. IBM. Tracor." He didn't dare hope too hard for any of them, though he thought he was qualified.

"How old are you?" she asked.

"Twenty-two," he said. "You?"

"Nineteen," she said. "I'm only starting my second year of college."

Gideon smiled at her and opened her door for her. "But you like it?"

"I love it," she said, her voice taking on new energy. "I'm going to be a lawyer." She held herself up tall and proud too, and Gideon found her so attractive in that moment.

"I bet you will be," he said, tipping his hat. "You go on,

now. I don't want your mother mad at me, because you're late."

Penny stepped between him and the door, and Gideon felt like he positively towered above her. She was petite and proper, charming and charismatic. She was everything he wanted on the outside, and he hoped to get to know her on the inside so he could determine if they could build a life together.

"See you at six-thirty," she said, and she got behind the wheel of the car, closed the door, and backed out of his driveway.

Gideon watched her go, both dogs coming to stand beside him. Mack whined, and he said, "Yeah, I wish she could stay longer too," as he reached down to pat the dog's head.

4

Penny shrugged into the blouse she'd just put the buttons on, and it felt good against her skin. "Momma!" she called as she left her bedroom. Down the hall, and then down the steps, Penny found her mother in the kitchen. She had a whisk in her hands and she was whipping up a huge bowl of eggs.

The Aarons family ate a lot of eggs, and Penny was glad she wouldn't be around for dinner tonight, though she did love her mother's sweet and savory scrambled egg sliders.

"What about this?" Penny asked, adjusting the white fabric so that it wasn't too far off her shoulder. Her mother wouldn't like that, and she already knew that Penny liked Gideon more than anyone she'd been out with that year. "Too plain?"

"It's lovely," Momma said. A fond look covered her

expression, and she left the whisk in the bowl to come around the counter. "Not everything has to be covered in a print."

"Prints are really popular right now," Penny said, looking down at the blouse. "I tried to dress it up with the ruffles and pleats." The blouse was really form-fitting, but with the extra fabric in the pleats that ran up her ribcage, she didn't feel like she was showing everything. "I do like it."

"It's adorable," Momma said, and Penny jerked her attention to her mother.

"I'm not a puppy, Mother," she said "And I don't want Gideon to think I'm adorable. I want him to think I'm *beautiful. Sophisticated*, even." Worry danced through her as she watched her mom fiddle with the fabric along her waist.

She'd barely made the blouse long enough, and she knew her mother didn't like that it barely sat along the waistband of her shorts. Penny wouldn't even be wearing these shorts, and the lower bellbottoms she was planning to wear would definitely show a little bit of her stomach. If she could get out of the house like that, it would be a miracle, and Penny had been praying for exactly that for the whole afternoon as she sat at the sewing machine.

"He's older than me, Momma. I don't want him to think I'm cute or adorable, like his little sister."

"Penny." Her mother smiled and shook her head. She reached out and tucked Penny's hair behind her ear. "You can be beautiful and pure, too. You'll be one of the smartest women he's ever met." She nodded like what she said was gospel law and turned back to the kitchen. "I think you should wear jeans with that shirt. You don't want to show too much skin. That doesn't say beautiful or sophisticated. That says desperate."

"I'm planning on wearing jeans," Penny said. "Or that green denim skirt I got a couple of months ago."

"Oh, that would be nice," she said, picking up the bowl again. "With the white sandals we got from Aunt Matilda."

"I'll go try them on," Penny said. She went back upstairs to try on the skirt and then the jeans. She normally paid attention to what she wore, sure. But not this much. She usually picked out something she felt confident and pretty in and deemed it good.

Gideon had introduced something new into her life she hadn't felt with a man in a while. Butterflies. Excitement. Nerves. *She* wanted to impress *him*. Truth be told, she was a little desperate to do exactly that.

She went with the jeans, because they were more fashionable than the skirt, with the flared bottoms and the slim fit through her hips and waist. They definitely made her look skinnier than she was, though she barely carried any extra weight.

The sandals couldn't be seen with the wide jeans, but Penny kept them on her feet anyway. She took care with her makeup, moving methodically to apply the right amount of color to her cheeks to make herself look older, but not like she was trying too hard.

Penny was trying hard, but she didn't want to *look* like she was.

She still had a few pieces of hair to iron straight when the doorbell rang. She sucked in a breath, her fingers slipping a little on the flat iron. She heard her mother's voice downstairs, as she'd pitched it up a little as she greeted Gideon.

"Calm down," Penny coached herself under her breath. He was just another man. She'd been out with dozens of them.

As she unplugged the hair iron and went downstairs, she had the very real thought that Gideon was anything but just another man. One step into the sitting room proved that, as she found him grinning at her mother and saying something that made her laugh.

Her father touched her waist, and Penny inched out of the way so he could meet Gideon too. Gideon's eyes met hers from across the room, and something locked in place between them. He shook her father's hand, his smile brilliant and filling the whole room, the whole house. He was charming and simply gorgeous in that dark cowboy hat, a short-sleeved, blue paisley shirt, and a pair of black pants.

When her parents turned back to her, Penny could see Gideon had charmed them to the gills. Even her father had a glow Penny rarely saw, and she smiled at her mother and father, and nodded as they went through the doorway and into the back of the house.

"Ready?" Gideon asked, tucking his hands into his pockets.

"Yes," Penny said. "I'm ready." She walked across the room toward him, expecting him to step back and open the front door so she could go through in front of him.

He didn't budge. Instead, he reached for her with both hands, and she put hers in his. "You look amazing," he said. "Stunning. Simply beautiful." He smiled at her, the energy snapping in his eyes making her own nerves vibrate even more.

"Thank you," she said, ducking her head. "You look very nice, too."

"This is my brother's shirt," he said with a chuckle. "He dates a lot more than I do." He released one of her hands and opened the door. Penny went outside first, never letting go of his hand.

"You don't date?" Penny asked once they were side-by-side, walking toward his truck. It was an older model and had probably been white once upon a time. It was more of a light gray now, with some chips down the side of it. She liked that he didn't exude money, because it meant he lived within his means.

"Not much, no," he said.

"Why not?"

"I don't know. Probably because I never really met anyone who made me want to shower twice in one day."

Penny burst out laughing, thrilled when he joined her. "Well, I'm glad I inspired that in you."

He opened her door for her, and Penny climbed into the cab of the truck, glad she'd chosen the pants over the skirt. Gideon rounded the front of the vehicle and got behind the wheel. "All right. There's a concert happening on Main Street tonight. It's a staged concert, so we get to hear one band at Miller's. They'll serve appetizers. Then we get twenty minutes to get to Kitty's Kitchen, where we get to see another local Texas band, and they'll serve a salad course there."

"I've heard of this," Penny said. "The progressive dinner and concert night. I didn't realize they were doing that in Sweet Creek."

"It's the first one," he said.

"How did you get tickets?" Penny had read in the paper several weeks ago that these progressive country music dinners sold out quickly, at least in places like Austin and San Antonio. The one she'd read about had been in Fredericksburg, which was a much bigger town in the Hill Country than Sweet Creek.

"I had to call in a favor," he said, glancing at her as he put the truck in drive after backing out. "But I got them, and I think it'll be an interesting experience."

"How many bands?" she asked.

"Four tonight," he said. "Appetizers, salad, main course, dessert. It'll be a couple of hours at least."

"I'm excited," she said. Number one, he'd planned a

real date. He'd showered—twice—and he'd come to her door to pick her up. As he rumbled down the road toward the highway, Penny shook her hair over her shoulders. "So, Gideon Walker, tell me what you want from life."

He looked at her, alarm in his expression. "What I want from life?"

"Yeah," she said.

"That's a huge thing," he said.

"Surely you have dreams and goals," she said. He certainly seemed like the type of man who would. Penny didn't want a handsome man on her arm who had no goals. "I'll go first, if you want."

"Sure," he said.

"I'm going to be one of the first female lawyers to graduate from UT-Austin," she said. "And I want to be a mother."

Gideon cleared his throat, and Penny wondered if she'd come on too strong. Again. "I remember the lawyer part," he said, shifting in his seat. He pulled up to the stop sign and looked at her instead of turning onto the highway. "How many children do you want?"

"As many as the Good Lord will give me," Penny said.

Gideon blinked, and Penny mentally kicked herself for being so bold. At the same time, she wanted to be herself, and she had no problem speaking her mind. If Gideon didn't like that...well, maybe this would be their first and last date.

Then a smile spread across his face, and he chuckled.

The sound grew and grew into a full, round laugh. He pulled onto the highway while his laughter lingered, and while Penny smiled, she didn't laugh with him.

"I like you, Penelope Aarons," he said. "You know what you want, that's for sure."

Penny folded her arms, unsure if he'd just complimented her or not. "What do you want?"

"I like technology," he said. "I have a degree in business, but what I really want to do is work in technology." He glanced at her. "You know, computers and stuff."

"I've heard of computers," she said dryly.

His grin didn't fade even one degree. "I'm sure you have."

"So you want to work in technology," she prompted.

"Yeah," he said. "In fact, earlier today, I applied to those places we talked about this morning."

Penny turned away from him and smiled out the passenger window. "That's great."

"Yeah, I'm just taking three classes in the fall, and I need a job."

"I'm assuming you work the ranch for your family in the summer?"

"Yes," he said. "It's enough to pay for a semester. I need to work to save for the next one, and to pay for my apartment and everything."

"Impressive," she said, and she was impressed by him. "Do you want a family?"

"Sure," he said. "Down the line."

"Down the line?"

"Yeah," he said. "When the time is right."

Penny watched him out of the corner of her eye, and he seemed perfectly comfortable with her. She liked that, liked the way he drove with one hand lazily draped over the steering wheel, liked that he fiddled with the radio to get it tuned in better.

"So you don't know what you want?" she asked.

"I need some time to boil it down," he said. "Can I have some time to think about it?"

"Sure," she said. "Of course."

"Great." He glanced at her. "I usually lead with easier questions, like, how many siblings do you have?" He grinned widely then, his teeth white and perfectly straight.

Penny giggled, glad everything between them was so easy. "I have three older brothers," she said. "I think you met Darren the other day when you stopped by." He nodded, so she kept going. "He's the oldest, and he's running our trucking operation right now. Brandon is next, and he's twenty-four and he runs the egg operation. He sells to the grocery stores and restaurants. All of that."

"Interesting," Gideon said.

"And Andrew is twenty-one, and he works the farm with my brothers and father. He wants to learn to drive one of the big rigs, but the school is expensive, and he hasn't taken that leap yet."

"And you want to be a lawyer," Gideon said. "That's

not anything like running an egg farm or a trucking business."

"Nope," she said. "I crate the eggs and feed a building of chickens and anything else that needs to be done. That way, I have the money I need to go to school."

"You love your family."

"Yes," she said. "You?"

"I do love my family," he said. "I'm the middle son, and my father recently transferred ownership of the ranch to Jonas, my older brother. Spencer is younger than me—just a year older than you—and he's not sure what he's going to do." Gideon sighed and rolled his right shoulder as if he'd hurt it recently. "He might stay on the ranch. There's room for another homestead. He might buy his own. He's not real keen on going to school."

"So you're not really like your family either," she said.

He came to the red light on the south end of town and turned to look at her. "I suppose so."

She smiled, and he returned the gesture, and the whole world could've wasted away and Penny wouldn't have known it. When Gideon looked at her, he was the only thing that mattered. He was the only thing she could focus on.

Someone honked, and Gideon flinched. He chuckled as he ducked his head and pressed on the accelerator to go through the light, which had turned green at some point. Heat moved through Penny, because when he looked at her, something obviously happened for him too, and she really liked that.

"All right," Gideon said as he turned into the parking lot at Miller's. "This looks fun."

An enormous tent had been set up in the back corner, and the moment Gideon opened his door, Penny heard guitars and drums. He came around and opened her door, and Penny slid to the pavement, immediately slipping her hand into his. Energy pulsed through the air, and Penny glanced around, trying to see everything at once.

When Gideon leaned down and asked, "It's gonna be crowded tonight. You okay to stay?" she felt alive in a brand-new way. She'd be okay if she was with Gideon. No matter what happened or where they went or how many people pressed in around them, if she could hold Gideon's hand, she'd be just fine.

5

Gideon stepped into the homestead to find his mother pouring herself a glass of ice tea. "Who's on the phone?" Gideon asked.

"I don't know," his mom said. "I didn't answer it. Spence did, but he went out to the front gate to meet the brickmason."

"Okay." He moved over to the kitchen sink to wash his hands before he went into the hall to take the call. His brother had hollered to him from the back porch about the call, and Gideon had finished filling the trough for the goats before he'd come in.

"This is Gideon Walker," he said a few seconds later, cradling the phone between his arm and shoulder while he finished drying his hands.

"Mister Walker," a man said. "This is Emmett Hard-grove from IBM."

Gideon dropped the kitchen towel. "Hi," he said. "Hello."

"I'm reviewing your application, and I wondered if you had a few minutes to answer some questions."

"Yeah," Gideon said. "Yes, of course." His heart raced in his chest, because out of the four companies he'd put in applications with, IBM was the biggest. They were the best. He wanted them the most.

They definitely had the technology he wanted to work with. They'd made more advancements than anyone else in the past few years, and his skin itched to be buzzed through those doors and to be present in their meetings.

He'd read everything he could get his hands on about the company, and they had manufacturing plants all over the world. They'd announced a new mainframe computer that could hold similar data in half the space. He'd heard rumblings of the company starting work on a line of personal computers, after the departure of one of their best minds had left to start his own company.

He wasn't even sure what questions Emmett asked, or how he answered, but before he knew it, the interview ended. Gideon hung up, his mind whirring. He hadn't been offered a job, but as he forced himself to slow down, he could hear how smart he'd sounded.

Emmett had said he'd call him the following day, and Gideon would probably be on a conference call with others in the company for a second interview.

"A second interview." A smile filled Gideon's whole

soul, and he paused in the hallway and closed his eyes. "Dear Lord, if at all possible, I would love this job at IBM."

"Gideon," Jonas barked, and Gideon ended the prayer there and stepped out of the hallway.

"Right here."

"We've got goats all over the ranch. You didn't close the gate."

"Shoot," Gideon said. "Sorry, I was in a hurry." He jogged through the kitchen and back outside to find the goats all over the garden and back yard. They'd eat everything in a matter of minutes, and he had no idea how long he'd been on the phone.

"Sorry," he said again as Jonas joined him.

"Must've been a really important phone call," his brother grumbled.

Gideon said nothing as he went with his brother to get some ropes out of the barn. Goats weren't nearly as stubborn as cattle, but it would be no picnic getting all these animals back where they belonged. Then he'd have to deal with his mother when she saw the state of her garden....

As Gideon worked, he thought about Penny and how she'd react completely different about the phone call when he told her about it that night. He let his imagination run through an amazing scenario where she laughed and congratulated him as he held her in his arms. Then he could lean down and kiss her....

The following evening, Gideon couldn't get to Penny's fast enough. The time since the interview had moved incredibly slowly, and he felt like his muscles had been hooked up to a powerful source of electricity.

He went too fast down the dirt road toward the egg farm and Penny's house, but he couldn't slow down. The dust behind him kicked up into a thick cloud, and her family probably wouldn't like breathing it for the next half an hour until it settled.

He forced himself to slow down as the big warehouse where Penny crated eggs came into view. He'd never been inside, but Penny had pointed it out to him on their second date. He'd had a third with her too, and tonight was their fourth.

He'd been nothing but the perfect Texas gentleman, but he really wanted to kiss Penny. Soon.

"You have to," he told himself. "Everything is about to change, and she has to know how you feel."

He pulled into her driveway, pleased when she stood from where she'd been sitting on the front steps. Gideon barely had time to flip the truck into park before he flew from it. "I got it," he called to her, already laughing. "I got the job, Pen." He jogged a few steps toward her, and she did the same to him until he swept her up into his arms, both of them laughing as he twirled her around.

He set her on her feet and looked down at her, gallons upon gallons of happiness pouring through him. "I got the job at IBM."

She clasped her hands behind his neck and gazed up at him with that soft, sexy smile on her face that he really liked. Really, really liked. "I knew you would," she said in that pretty little voice of hers. "They'd be stupid not to hire you."

Gideon just grinned, because her confidence in him felt so good. "I think I might know what I want now," he said.

"Oh, do tell," Penny said, dropping her hands from around his neck and taking one of his as she strolled back toward his truck.

He squeezed her fingers. "I want to invent something. Something big. I want to work in technology, with computers, with the space program. Or the banking business—did you read that article I left with you about the automated machines in England? The networks for banking are going to be *huge*. And we'll need security for all of that, and I want to do that. I want to learn about all of it, and *do* something no one's ever done before."

He took a big breath and held it to calm himself down. At the same time, his determination and desire to be someone important and color outside the lines was a real driving force in his life, one he thought was good.

Penny got in the truck while he held the door for her, and he stepped into the space between the door and the truck while she buckled her seat belt. "And Pen, I want to be a father too."

She clicked the belt into place and swung her attention toward him. "Is that right?"

"Yeah," he said, grinning. He closed the door though she looked like she had something more to say. Once behind the wheel, he said, "Go on and ask."

"Ask what?"

"You know what." He flipped the truck into reverse and backed out of her driveway.

"How many kids do you want?" she asked.

"As many as the Good Lord will give me," he said.

She giggled, and Gideon could only look at her. She wore her hair curled tonight, clipped back on the sides to reveal more of her gorgeous face. She wore makeup, but not so much that Gideon couldn't see her natural beauty.

He'd learned a lot about her on their previous three dates, and he liked everything that came out of her mouth. He liked her parents, and he liked that she didn't mind working.

"It's going to take a lot of time to handle as many kids as God will give you," Penny said, something forced about her voice. "How will you balance that and being the world's next great inventor?"

"I—" Gideon found his explanation fleeing. He had no idea, because he didn't think about stuff like this. He didn't have to, because he wasn't married. He didn't have a wife with a child on the way. He didn't even have a career yet.

"I'll figure it out," he said, because Gideon knew he

could. He was smart too, and he would find a way to juggle a wife, family, and a career in technology. "There is a little snag in all this good news."

He cleared his throat, and the mood in the cab changed instantly.

"What's that?" she asked.

"They want me there on the twenty-eighth."

"Of July?"

"Yes," he said.

"Gideon," she said. "That's only nine days from today."

"Yeah," he said. "I know." He looked out his window and then back to the road in front of him. "I'm moving to Austin next weekend, Penny."

She didn't answer, and when he dared to look over to her, he found her with her arms folded, looking out her window. "Are you breaking up with me then?" she asked.

"No," he said quickly, surprised she'd even asked. "No, of course not." He pulled over to the side of the road, because this conversation required his full attention. "Penny," he said gently. "Will you look at me, sweetheart?"

She did, her eyes wide and worried. He liked that she was strong, and smart, and soft all at the same time.

"I don't want to break up," he said. "I'll only be in Austin for three weeks until you come. It's three weeks, and I'll have a phone. We can call at night, and there's no reason for us to break up when you'll be in Austin in only three weeks." He gave her a small smile. "What do you think? Do you want to break up with me?"

She shook her head. "Three weeks?"

"Three weeks," he said. "And hey, we still have nine more days before I have to go. Well, I'll move on Saturday. So I guess only seven days." One week. It wasn't long enough, not for Gideon. As he gazed at Penny, he had the very real impression that seven days with him wasn't long enough for Penny either.

"My parents want you to come for dinner," Penny said, blinking and the vulnerability in her eyes disappearing. Now she wore a sparkle, along with an edge of wariness.

"Oh," he said. "Okay." He straightened and checked his rear-view mirror. He eased back onto the highway and asked, "When?"

"At your earliest convenience," she said. "That's actually what my father said." She giggled, and that eased some of Gideon's anxiety. He wasn't even sure what he was worried about. He'd met her parents before, both of them. Her mother a couple of times, and her father just the first time he'd gone to pick her up last week.

"I'll come to dinner at the farmhouse," he said. "But you have to do something for me too."

"Is that right?" she teased. "And what would that be?"

"Show me that duck pond you've been tellin' me about for a week."

She burst out laughing, and Gideon joined in with

her. They had fun together, and Gideon liked that. They'd talked about serious things too, and he'd enjoyed those talks too. Penny made him think, and he'd never met a woman who'd done that.

He'd never met a woman like her at all, and though she was young, she seemed to have so much figured out.

"I can show you the pond," she said. "You'll have to come a few minutes early."

"Deal," he said. The conversation moved on to other things—his class schedule and who her roommates would be when she moved to Austin—but Gideon's thoughts revolved around how he could kiss her good-night when he dropped her off after their date that evening.

"Gideon Walker, you did not get us tickets to the Summer Square dance Spectacular." Penny clapped her hand over her mouth and looked at him.

"What?" he asked in mock sarcasm. "You don't want to go to this? Funny, I swear you mentioned it about fifty times after church on Sunday." He chuckled as she swatted at his chest.

"I can't believe you," she said. "This has been sold out for months." She looked at him, searching his face. "How did you get tickets to this? And do not say you had to call in a favor."

Gideon cocked his eyebrows at her and pulled into the parking space where the lot usher indicated he should. "I don't know what to say now."

"How do you know so many people?" she asked.

"My brother's girlfriend works for the county events office," he said. "They usually have extra tickets to things all over the county, and they sometimes get tickets for themselves that they don't use. I called her as soon as I got home after dropping you off on Sunday. She asked around the office, and she actually came up with five or six tickets that wouldn't be used."

"This is unbelievable," Penny said as Gideon got out of the truck. She waited for him to open the door, and she stepped right into his arms. "Thank you, Gideon." She was sincere, and the world narrowed to just the two of them despite the crowd around them.

Tonight, she wore a yellow pair of pants, with a white, blue, red, and yellow striped sweater that hugged her arms to her elbows. She'd put a wide, white belt around her waist, and Gideon felt like the luckiest man in the county to be with her.

"Come on, sweetheart," he said, stepping back. He wanted to kiss her, but not here. Not in front of anyone and everyone streaming by, not when he couldn't take his time and truly experience her. "Tonight, we get to dance our cares away."

6

Penny reached up and pushed her hair off her sweaty forehead with the back of her hand. The eggs just kept coming and coming, and she was tired. She'd promised her late nights with Gideon wouldn't interfere with her work, though, so she hadn't dared to even whisper a complaint.

She got up on time. She came to the egg warehouse on time. She worked through the morning, no matter how hot it got in the warehouse.

Today she was crating eggs into the dozen retail packages, and she did love the recyclable cartons that were made from grass. They usually made her smile, as did the multi-colored eggs that came through the opening in the wall on the conveyor belt.

She'd been crating eggs since the age of seven, and it wasn't particularly hard work. She remembered the anxiety when she'd first started and how gingerly she'd touched the eggs. They were tougher than they looked, and it actually took a lot to break an egg with her bare hands. She really only ran into a problem when they fell on the floor.

The tracks were in place though, and it really was impossible for them to fall—unless she let them get so backed up that they pushed through the openings on the ends of the belt. She sometimes dropped them, because she'd learned to pick up three eggs at a time and *drop, drop, drop*, set them in the cartons.

She finished the row of five she'd been working on, and her hands just knew what to do next. She flipped the tops over and secured them in place, then deftly stacked the cartons on top of one another. After pushing them into place against the others she'd already filled, Penny turned to get more cartons.

Five fit here, no matter how many times she tried to make six fit. She'd given up on trying to squeeze in an extra carton, because it always ended in disaster.

She didn't particularly enjoy the retail dozen crating, because she had to inspect the eggs too. They were washed when they did retail crating, and sometimes the eggs were more slippery than normal. Sometimes she wore rubber gloves to give herself some grip, but today, they'd only made her hands too sweaty inside the gloves, and she'd peeled them off after only fifteen minutes.

The eggs kept coming and coming, and Penny kept

crating and crating. Because the work didn't require a lot of mental energy, her mind was free to think about Gideon. The man was absolutely maddening, and Penny sighed as she remembered the feather-light touch of his hands on her waist as they'd danced last night.

He was maddening, because he was good at everything he did. She had no idea a man his size could be so agile, and when she asked him where he'd learned to dance, he'd said his grandmother had taught him in the kitchen at the homestead.

That only made him more endearing, and Penny had started to wonder if she had any endearing qualities. She knew she was pretty, but she wanted to be more than pretty. She knew she was smart, but honestly, most men didn't want a woman smarter than them. Gideon didn't seem to have a problem with it at all, and when she'd argued back with him about what she thought should happen with the county elections, he hadn't gotten his feelings hurt and shut the conversation down.

He'd interacted with her like her opinions were important and valid. The conversation had been stimulating for her, and she hoped for him too.

"What else?" she asked herself, her voice barely loud enough to be heard over the low hum of the conveyor belt and the mechanical sounds that came from further in the warehouse. "There has to be more to you than a pretty face and quick wit."

She could dance too, and she did put together a good

meal. She loved to sew, and she could see all the straight lines and hems of a garment before she even started.

So you have some skills, she thought, finally leaving that topic behind.

Gideon was strong. He worked hard around his family's ranch. He'd already earned one degree, and he'd gotten a job at IBM. Every time he showed up at her house, he was clean-cut, polished, and polite. He definitely had all the right pieces in all the right places.

And yet, he was utterly maddening, because he hadn't kissed her when he'd dropped her off last night. True, Darren had just arrived back at the farmhouse too, and he'd walked with the two of them up the sidewalk to the porch.

But Gideon hadn't even climbed the steps. Darren had, and he'd gone inside, leaving Penny and Gideon alone. The porch light had haloed the two of them, and under the starry, Texas sky, the desire to kiss him had reached a new level.

He'd said, "Thanks for a great night, Pen. I'll call you tomorrow." He'd hugged her quickly, whispering, "I don't want your brother to watch our first kiss. Tomorrow?" before stepping back.

What was she supposed to say to that? She'd just nodded and gone up the steps and into the house. Darren was loitering in the sitting room, and Penny had swatted him with both hands. "You ruined it," she'd hissed to keep her voice low. She didn't need to wake her parents over a kiss she still hadn't gotten. "Why couldn't you have been five minutes earlier? Or five minutes later?"

Darren had shrunk back and held up his arms, though she wasn't hitting him hard enough to even hurt. He'd chuckled—actually chuckled—and said, "If I was five minutes later, I'd have totally interrupted you kissing him."

Penny stood back, searching his face. "What?"

"Oh, Pen," Darren said, smiling for all he was worth. "That man is smitten with you. When he kisses you, it's not going to be a quick thing."

Penny hadn't known what to say to that. She was already late coming home, and she'd laid in bed for at least an hour, thinking about the kiss she'd hoped and prayed for that she hadn't quite gotten yet.

"Tomorrow night," she vowed as she filled the fifth egg carton. Lids closed. Cartons stacked and moved out of the way. More cartons laid out. She was going to kiss him tomorrow night when he came for dinner at the farmhouse. She'd spoken briefly with her mother that morning, and they'd agreed on dinner then.

Later today, Penny would see Gideon after church, and she hoped he'd invite her to the potluck picnic that followed the sermon. If he didn't, she was planning to invite him. She couldn't kiss him in front of all the little old ladies at the potluck though, and if she snuck off with the man, her brothers would tease her relentlessly.

She wasn't sure why she cared what they thought of

her. She knew Gideon was far different than anyone else she'd ever dated, and that turned her thoughts to the future. As a little girl, she'd fantasized about three things: the day she passed the state bar and became a lawyer, her wedding day, and becoming a mother.

Though she'd only just begun a relationship with Gideon, it already felt serious to her. All of a sudden, she wasn't sure how to be all of the things she'd always wanted to be. Did women raise a family and practice law at the same time? Which did she want more, and was she willing to give up one for the other?

New fantasies had started to bloom in her mind, and they all featured dark-haired, dark-eyed boys and girls. Spitting images of Gideon, with his quick smile and loud laugh.

"He won't even kiss you," she said, frustration building in her chest again. Having his children seemed so far away, and yet, her mind had started to revolve around what her future actually held.

The door opened, and Penny looked up as Andrew came in with a couple of other workers. "Almost done," he said. "How many have we got?"

"Five hundred," Penny said. She'd been crating so long, she had a feel for what she'd done. That, and she grouped the cartons in stacks of five and rows of twenty. The table had been marked with tape for this purpose exactly, and she'd just finished her fifth section. "They're still coming."

"We just finished the washing," he said, pulling a cart over to the long, steel table where she crated. "They'll be done in ten minutes." He started loading the cartons onto the cart, as did Phillip and Luke. They loaded the cartons so much faster than she'd been able to do herself, and it was almost disheartening to see an entire morning's worth of work get taken so quickly.

Andrew started cleaning up while Phillip and Luke took the cart out to the van. They'd deliver the eggs that afternoon, and they'd be in the refrigerated cases in the stores by that evening. Penny did enjoy seeing her family's eggs in the grocery store, though she never bought eggs. They had plenty of fresh eggs whenever they wanted them.

She'd begged her mother not to do an egg dish for tomorrow night's dinner, and her mom said she'd look through her recipes.

The eggs finally stopped, and Penny finished with 3 eggs in one of the cartons. She took them back out, because they didn't waste cartons, and they didn't sell partials. She'd take these back to the house, where she'd have to rush to get ready for church.

"Thanks for helping clean up," she said to Andrew, who just nodded. They walked back to the farmhouse together, and Penny wondered why he was so quiet. As they went down the slight rise, she asked, "Are you okay, Andy?"

"I need your help," he said, slowing his step until he

stopped. Penny did the same, passing him one of the eggs to carry. "I want to talk to Dad about going to school."

Penny wasn't sure what she'd expected her brother to say—maybe that he'd met a girl and wanted help asking her out—but it wasn't that. "Oh," she said. "Why are you asking me?"

"Because you're the only one of us who's gone to college." Andy looked at her then, and she saw the unrest in her brother's soul. "I want to study accounting and run the financial side of the egg farm."

"I thought you wanted to go to truck driving school."

"I don't want to be on the road my whole life," he said, toeing the ground with his boot. "See, I met this girl, and she's making me re-think things."

"A girl?" Penny asked, linking her arm through Andy's. "We have to go, or Momma will be out here yelling at us to hurry up. Church starts in less than an hour." She deliberately didn't ask who he'd met, because Andy would usually tell without being asked if left alone.

"Yeah," Andy said. "And I know I'm not as smart as you, but I've always liked math, and I think I could earn a certificate or something to be able to keep working the farm—I don't want to give that up—but not have to be on the road for nine months out of the year."

"You're plenty smart," she said. "You'd do great at college." They went up the front steps together, and Penny paused, despite the risk of incurring her mother's wrath. "You just go up to Daddy, and you say, 'Daddy, I've been thinking, and I've found this great accounting program.' You have to find the program first, Andy. Do the research. I can help you before I go back to Austin."

"Okay," he said. "I don't think I can leave Sweet Creek. There have to be things closer around here."

"I'm sure there are," she said. "We'll find out. Anyway, then you tell him what you want to do, and here's the key, Andy. You ask *him* what he thinks. Ask him for his advice. Daddy loves to give advice, and honestly, he's not wrong very often."

Andrew nodded and reached to open the door with the words, "Thanks, Pen. Can we start looking around this week?"

She hadn't told anyone but her mother that Gideon was leaving town on Saturday, and she opened her mouth to say she might be busy, as she wanted to spend every spare moment with him before he left, but her mother yanked open the door.

Her bright green eyes blazed with unhappy fire. "There you two are. We have to leave in twenty minutes. You know better than to dawdle on the Sabbath."

"Sorry, Momma," Andrew mumbled as he stepped past her.

Penny simply smiled at her mom and asked, "What did you decide on for dinner tomorrow night?"

"Oh, do you think about anything but that boy?" Momma asked, shooing Penny into the house. Penny only giggled, because she knew her mother liked Gideon

Walker a whole lot. Not as much as Penny, but a whole lot, and she'd definitely make a spectacular dinner for "that boy."

———

Penny sat on the front steps, looking down the road despite the fact that she heard nothing.

Gideon was late. Her left leg bounced as she tried to get her nerves out before he got there. If he was even coming.

With every minute that passed, she saw her opportunity to take him down to the duck pond and kiss him shrink right before her eyes.

Just then, the familiar rumble of an engine filled the air, and in the next moment, Gideon's dirty-white truck came into view. By the time he pulled into her driveway, Penny stood at the end of the sidewalk, every nerve ending buzzing with excitement.

"I'm so sorry," he said as he got out of the truck. She met him at the front of it, no way to smother her smile. He drew her into his embrace as he explained further. "I got into it with Jonas, and my father doesn't let us just walk away angry."

He pulled back and sighed. "So we had to have this talk, and...." His voice trailed off as he shook his head. "It's fine. I'm here." He met her eyes. "Do we still have time to see the pond?"

"Let me check with my mom real quick, okay?" She darted into the garage and went up the steps. She walked past the laundry room, the scent of cooking beef filling her nose. "Momma, Gideon just got here, and I want to show him the duck pond. Are we okay to head over there for a bit?"

Her mother looked over her shoulder. "That's fine, dear." She smiled at Penny. "Daddy just radioed in to say he needs a few extra minutes, so there's time."

Relief filled Penny, and she nodded. She hurried across the kitchen and kissed her mom's cheek. "I think he's finally going to kiss me, Momma."

Her mother laughed lightly and said, "Be gentle with him, Pen."

"I will," Penny promised, and she hurried back outside to Gideon. "We're good for a bit," she said. "Daddy said he needs a few extra minutes out with the chickens."

"Great." Gideon laced his fingers through hers, and they started up the road. About halfway to the egg warehouse, she deviated off the road and down a path that was barely noticeable.

"I love coming here," Penny said, letting go of his hand so she could walk ahead of him. The path was only wide enough for one, and Penny's soul quieted as the pond expanded before her.

"Why?" Gideon asked. "What's special about it?"

Penny paused on the path to take in the trees, the lush green grass, and the still water. A duck even quacked in the silence. "It's just so peaceful," she said. "Whenever I'm not sure what to do, I come here, because it's easy to think."

She continued down the path, wishing she had more time to sit on the bench beside the pond and do exactly what she'd just said. Think. She needed some clarity of mind as she started to think about what her future truly held for her.

She reached the bottom of the path, and Gideon stepped beside her. "I feel like I've gotten a lot of answers here." She took a deep breath and looked at him.

"It's beautiful," he said, still surveying the pond.

"I came here when my grandmother died, and I came when I was trying to decide where to go to school. The duck pond never lets me down." She hoped the magic and charm of it would earn her a kiss today.

Gideon looked at her, and they seemed to be of one mind. He took her into his arms, and she ran her hands up his arms to his face. "I sure do like you, Penny," he said, his voice as quiet and peaceful as the duck pond.

"I sure like you too," she whispered. "If you don't kiss me right now, I might go crazy."

He chuckled and ducked his head, causing the brim of his cowboy hat to bump her forehead. He swept the hat off his head, and Penny let her eyes drift closed. Her pulse raced in anticipation, and she drew in a breath that held the uniquely masculine scent of Gideon. Leather and cotton and soap and spicy musk.

His lips touched hers, and while he wasn't the first boy Penny had kissed, he was definitely the first man. She cradled his face in her hands as he slowly kissed her, then moved her fingers into his hair as she matched his movement. She didn't want to be gentle; she wanted him to know how much she liked him and how much she didn't want him to leave on Saturday.

By the time he pulled away, Penny had lost all track of time. The world swayed behind her closed eyes, and she tucked herself against his chest so she could feel his heartbeat.

Everything in her life shifted again, because she now knew she wanted Gideon Walker to be part of her future, and that meant other pieces had to be shifted around.

After a few more minutes, Penny said, "We better get back to the farmhouse."

"All right," he said. "Just one more thing." Then he kissed her again, and Penny melted right into his touch as he embedded himself in her heart.

7

Gideon hadn't kissed a woman in a long time, but thankfully, he still knew how to do it. At least Penny seemed to like it. His stomach still clenched with nerves, because he'd only gotten one thing out of the way—kissing Penny.

Now he had to go to dinner with her family. His argument with Jonas lingered in the back of his mind, and he wished he'd been able to control his tongue and his temper. He didn't need that added stress in his life right now.

But he honestly didn't care if Jonas needed to hire someone for the ranch sooner than he'd expected. It was his ranch, and he had to shoulder the responsibility for it. His father hadn't been happy with Gideon's argument either, but what did they expect?

"You gave *him* the ranch," Gideon had said, his voice too loud. "What do you want from me? My blood, sweat, and tears until the day I die? *This isn't my ranch*—as you've both made very clear. This isn't my responsibility, and I'm not going to feel guilty because I have to go to Austin to start a job with literally the best technology firm in the state. I'm not."

He'd tried to leave then, but his mother had given him a cocked-eyebrow look that said, *Sit down, Gideon.*

So he'd sat back down.

He put the conversation out of his mind and focused on the feel of Penny's hand in his. "They're going to like me, right?" he asked, usually not so nervous when he was with Penny. But he hadn't met a woman's parents before, and while Penny's mother was nice, her father had definitely sized up Gideon every time he looked at him.

"Of course they are," Penny said, nudging him with her shoulder. "Don't tell me you're seriously worried about it."

"I'm definitely worried about it." Gideon gazed out over the fields surrounding the buildings they were passing. "Is this where your chickens live?"

"That's right," she said. "We have thirty thousand *layer hens*. Not chickens."

"Holy cow," he said. "How many do you feed?"

"I only have to do building six," she said. "It takes about an hour in the evening. You can come help me tonight." She grinned up at him and giggled. "Isn't this the most romantic date you've ever been on? Dinner with your girlfriend's parents and feeding chickens." She laughed, and Gideon could smile with her. If he was with Penny, he didn't much care what they did.

"We have all this land too," Penny said. "Because we have to let our hens out during the day. They're free range."

"And you gather them all up at night?"

"Birds like to roost at night," she said. "They come in themselves, and Brandon rides around on an ATV and gathers up the stragglers. They get fed, and in the morning, we gather their eggs. And we have a crew who gathers in the afternoon too. Hens don't really care what our schedule is."

"I bet they don't." Gideon's stomach swooped as the farmhouse came into view. He took in a deep breath and tried to tell himself that he'd be fine. Penny would be there, and surely her father and brothers wouldn't fire questions at him that he couldn't answer.

"My father loves talking mechanical stuff," Penny said. "And you can't go wrong with my mom if you compliment her cooking."

"Mechanical stuff," Gideon said. "Does that extend to technology?"

Penny pealed out a string of laughter. "No, sir. It does not." She looked up at him. "My dad is awesome. Great.

But he's literally worked on this egg farm since he was six years old. He's smart, and he's made some great improvements around here. His main goal is to make sure this place can continue into the future for his sons."

"Got it," Gideon said, his mind moving through the things she'd told him.

Before he knew it, Penny was leading him up the steps to the deck attached to the back of the house, and then she opened the door. Cool air met them, and Gideon started to relax a little bit.

"There they are," her mother said, her voice falsely bright. Penny's hand in his tightened, and he stepped to her side.

All three of her brothers stopped what they were doing and looked at him. Gideon worked not to clear his throat or shift his feet. Darren set down the fork in his hand and straightened, but Gideon was still a couple of inches taller than him.

They all sported hair in various shades of brown, with plenty of that auburn mixed in that Penny had too. Her mother came around the counter and said, "Stop staring at him."

"My brothers," Penny blurted, as if her mother's voice had thawed something inside her. "Darren's the oldest." She nodded to him. "I think you've met him before."

"Sure have," Gideon said, putting a smile on his face as he stepped forward to shake her brother's hand. "And you must be Brandon," he added, glancing at Penny, who loitered near the door, watching him. "And the youngest is Andrew."

"Penny's the youngest," Darren said.

"The youngest boy, he meant," Penny said with a bit of bite in her voice.

Gideon shook all of their hands, glad when they smiled back at him and gripped his fingers with strength.

"My mother," Penny said. "You've met, but formally, this is Jean. Where's Daddy?"

"He—" her mother started.

"Right here," her father said, and Gideon turned toward the sound of his voice. He came out of the doorway, and he alone had purely brown hair and dark eyes. The boys had a mix of hazel and green eyes, and Penny was the only one with the bright pair her mother had.

"My father," Penny said. "Jason Aarons. Daddy, Momma, this is Gideon Walker."

"I think I've heard that name before," Jason said, and Gideon chuckled. "Penny doesn't usually hold a whole lot back, in case you haven't figured that out."

"Daddy," Penny said. "You said you wouldn't embarrass me."

"At least we like this one," Darren said.

"Darren," Penny hissed.

"Let's sit down," Jean chirped. "Boys, behave."

Shuffling and the scraping of chairs, and Gideon sat beside Penny while the brothers took up places across from them. Her father settled at one end of the table, and her mom turned back to the kitchen.

"I'm just saying," Brandon said. "Gideon seems normal. Remember that one guy who didn't know Mississippi was a state?"

"Are you really going to do this?" Penny asked as her brothers twittered with laughter. "Because, if I recall, Brandon, you went out with that girl from—"

"Stop it," Brandon said, not laughing anymore. He glanced at his father and back to Penny, the message clear.

"I'm just saying," she said. "I know plenty about you too." She glared at him and then switched her gaze to Darren. "I could say plenty about you too."

"Hey," he protested. "I said I liked him."

"I like him too," Andrew said quickly, and Gideon wondered what dirt Penny had on him.

Her mother set a pot roast on the table, complete with carrots and potatoes in the stock. Gideon's mouth watered, and he smiled at her mom. "This looks amazing, ma'am."

"I just need to get the butter out of the microwave oven." She hurried away, and Gideon swung his attention after her.

"You have a microwave oven?" He half-rose from his seat, bumping the table. Heat filled his face, but he couldn't stop himself. He straightened fully as he watched her mom open the microwave oven that sat right there on the counter. How he hadn't seen it escaped him, but he could now.

"Did you guys see the demos they did at Fischer's?" he asked. "Is that where you got it?" In that moment, he realized that everyone was staring at him. "I mean, I wanted my mother to get one, but she's not a fan."

"Gideon likes technology," Penny said.

"Yes," her father said. "He's got a job at IBM."

Gideon swung his attention to Jason, and he caught the smile on his face before it slid away. He sat down and glanced at Darren, who simply looked back at him.

"Okay," Jean said, returning to the table. She set a bowl of mostly melted butter in the middle of it. "Uh, I'm still figuring it out." She sat down, the tension in the room now as thick as breathing through cotton.

Gideon started chuckling, the sound low in his throat but gaining strength and volume. Jason joined in, and that somehow gave everyone at the table permission to laugh too, even Jean.

"Stop it," she said between her giggles, but she beamed at Gideon like he was her personal Savior. Everything after that was easy, and Gideon enjoyed himself—and the food, and the company he was with—a whole lot.

He'd kissed the woman, and he liked her family. After they fed the chickens—oops, layer hens—and after he'd kissed her good-bye and driven away, Gideon wondered why he was moving to Austin this weekend.

Penny obviously had plenty of male admirers, and maybe she'd meet someone more interesting than him in the three weeks it took for her to follow him to school.

He lifted the last box into the back of his truck and turned back to Mack and Moose. The dogs sat on the porch and gazed down at him, clearly not happy that he was leaving. "I have to go, guys," he said, climbing the steps. He pushed Mack over and sat between them. "Daddy's still going to be here, and he's your real master."

Moose laid his head down in Gideon's lap, and he absently stroked the dog's head. His father had helped with the first few boxes, but there was work to do around the ranch every day of the week, even Saturday, and his father didn't like goodbyes, so he'd made an excuse about being needed in the stable, hugged Gideon, and left.

Jonas hadn't stuck around to help that morning, and Gideon wasn't surprised. He'd barely said two words to his brother since the argument on Monday night. Spencer had been working until Gideon said, "There's only one left, and I can get it."

He'd gone back inside with Gideon, but he'd gone into the kitchen while Gideon had gone back to his bedroom.

The front door opened behind him, and Gideon twisted to see his mother exiting the house. She groaned as she toed Mack out of the way and sat on the step beside him. She patted Gideon's knee and said, "You've got everything?"

"Yes, ma'am."

"Why are you still sittin' on the porch?"

Gideon smiled at her. "I don't know. Maybe I was hoping my momma would pack me a lunch so I wouldn't starve on moving day."

She laughed as she shook her head, and Gideon chuckled with her. "There's food inside, baby," she said. "All yous need to do is come get it." She stood up, while Gideon grinned at the plural use of you. Jonas talked the same way, and it did endear them to Gideon.

He followed her inside, picked up the brown paper bag she'd filled with food, and turned to hug her. "I love you, Momma."

"I love you too, Gideon." She stretched up to hold him, and he thought he'd never be too old to get a hug from his mother. "You be a good boy in Austin, okay?"

"Okay, Momma." He was tired of telling her he wasn't a boy anymore. To her, he'd always be her boy. "I can call you tonight?"

"Of course, baby," she said. "Call and tell me how the house is."

"I will." Gideon left then, because if he didn't, he didn't think he'd go at all. Driving away from the ranch was easy. Leaving Sweet Creek when Penny was still here was much harder than Gideon anticipated.

His nerves followed him all the way to Austin, because he'd rented a little house over the phone, sight unseen. He drove around in circles for a few minutes, but when he finally pulled up to the house, he was pleasantly surprised.

The lawn was green and trimmed. The white siding

on the house was actually white, and the driveway didn't hold any weeds. "Thank you, Lord," he whispered to the windshield. He had so much to be grateful for, and Gideon bowed his head and said a prayer of gratitude before he got out of the truck to go see where he'd be living for the foreseeable future.

8

Penny giggled, wishing she could get further from the kitchen. Her parents both sat at the dining room table, the ledgers where they kept their finances for the farm spread in front of them. They did this once a month, and Penny had made double chocolate brownies for the occasion.

They poured over the books for two or three nights, entering receipts and logging deposits. Every time they did, Penny was reminded of how much her mother and father loved one another, and that always warmed her heart.

Gideon's voice on the other end of the phone line helped with that too. "So you'll be livin' with a couple of other girls?" he asked. He'd called every night since he'd left Sweet Creek, and Penny liked that he operated like clockwork.

"Yes," she said, keeping her voice low. He'd told her about the job, and his voice always grew in volume and excitement when he detailed his desk at IBM, and talked about his boss, and the technology he was learning about. Oh, the technology.

Microchips that were shrinking but holding more data. Personal computers—which Gideon was convinced would be in homes one day. She couldn't imagine such a thing. Her mother could barely get the microwave oven to work, how would someone like her use a computer?

Besides, computers were bulky and filled entire rooms. Penny had marveled at the things Gideon had said about using the machines for the space program, for banking, for travel, for literally everything.

I'm telling you, Pen, he'd said. *This is going to be huge, and I can't wait for my chance to do something that will change the world.*

He spoke about credit cards and bank cards and the need to ensure encryption and security for people as they started shopping with plastic. He told her about Intel, a company that was preparing to announce "something huge" in the industry, and how he was right there, watching it all happen.

The man loved technology, and he thought in ways Penny couldn't comprehend. She adored the way he was passionate about something, and she had the very real feeling that if their relationship succeeded and she married him, she'd never live a boring life.

She wanted that with everything inside her. She loved her family and the egg farm, but she was a lot like Gideon in that she wanted more. She wanted to see and experience everything, and she knew Gideon did too.

"Who are they?" he asked, and Penny blinked to get herself back in the moment.

"There will be four of us," she said. "Last year, I lived with Hannah and Sherryl. We got along really great, so in the spring, we signed a contract for this apartment fairly close to campus. I'll share a room with Hannah."

"I can't wait to meet them," he said, and he wasn't lying. Gideon liked everyone he met, which was also something Penny liked about him.

She pressed her back into the wall in the hall, the phone cord stretched as far as she could get it. The constant tension made her arm ache, but she still sighed happily. "We thought it would be just the three of us, but then we got a letter a couple of weeks ago that a woman named Giselle will be in the apartment too. I don't know her."

"Hopefully she'll get along with the three of you," Gideon said. He yawned, and Penny took that as a cue that he needed to go.

"I'll let you go," she said. "You sound tired."

"No," he said. "Don't go. I'm fine."

Penny closed her eyes and leaned her head back against the wall. *Don't go.* He sounded somewhat desperate to keep her on the line, though they'd been talking for an hour.

"My mother is going to come around the corner at any moment and make me get off the phone anyway," Penny whispered.

"I want every second then," Gideon said, his voice almost as soft though he lived alone in a real house, in a real neighborhood, much farther from campus than Penny would. He had a vehicle though, and only planned on going to campus two days a week. She'd take her bicycle and ride the bus everywhere.

"Tell me about the chickens," he said.

She smiled, feeling herself sink further in love with this man. She wasn't sure what exactly it was about him, though he did exhibit kindness and genuine interest in her and what she was interested in. Perhaps that was it. He wasn't constantly talking about himself and how amazing he was, but he asked her about her life too.

"The chickens are boring," she said.

"Tell me what you're worried about then."

She opened her eyes, wondering how he'd known some of her doubts had been crowding back inside her mind. "I've got this advanced chemistry class this semester," she said. "I'm worried about that."

"You don't have to earn a degree in chemistry to go to law school," Gideon said. "You could switch to history, Pen. Or English. You might like that better."

"I might," she conceded. "But Gideon, I want...." She

didn't know how to say it without sounding too full of herself.

"You want to be the best," he said for her.

She couldn't deny it, so she stayed silent.

"You want to change the world," he said with a light laugh that made her heart ache. She wanted to be with him so badly, and she had no idea how she was going to survive the next two weeks.

"I think that's you, Mister Walker," she teased. If she didn't turn this moment light, she feared she might cry. And she would not waste one second of her phone call with Gideon crying. "What with your talk of cyber-something, and fiber optics, and micro...process...ing."

He burst out laughing, and the simple sound of that filled her spirit to the brim. When she missed him this week, she could remember this laugh and she'd be okay.

"It's a microprocessor, Pen," he said, still chuckling.

"Gideon, I miss you," Penny said, and he stopped laughing.

"I miss you too, sweetheart," he said. "No one's asked you out while I've been gone, right?"

She giggled again, because it was cute how much he wanted her to himself. "No, sir," she said. "I haven't even left the farm."

"That's good," he said. "I've been thinking, Pen...."

"Sounds dangerous," she teased.

Gideon remained silent, and Penny regretted that she hadn't just let him speak. "Go on," she said.

"I'm trying to find the right order for the words."

Penny's heartbeat sped. "What's it about?"

"Us," he said.

"What about us?" She stretched her legs out in front of her to get some relief in her tailbone. Everything was starting to go numb, and she'd need to stand up soon.

"I've just been thinkin' about...things," he said. "And how I'm going to balance it all."

"Your classes and work?"

"Yes, that," he said. "But farther down the road than that, sweetheart. I've only ever known ranch life. My dad worked all the time. Literally, all the time. He still does. Jonas does. Your father does too. How do they have families and faith and, I don't know, just do everything?"

"I don't know."

"Remember how you asked me what I wanted?"

"Yes."

"I want to do what's right," he said. "I want to be a good father, and a good husband, but I don't know what either of those really mean. What makes a good dad, you know? How can I be a good husband?" He paused for a moment. "And yes, I want to change the world. I want to be right there on the edge of everything new in the world, and I fear that might take me from my wife and family."

Penny let his words sink into her ears and mind. "It's about choices, Gideon," she said. "You have to prioritize things, that's all."

"A man needs to make a living for his family," he

argued back, though his voice was soft. "That requires him to be gone—a lot. Does that make him a bad father? A negligent husband?"

"Of course not," Penny said. "You'll—"

"Penny," her mother said. "Time to get off the phone."

She glanced up at her mom and nodded. She got to her feet as she said, "My mom wants me to get off, Gideon." She took a step toward her mom and then turned her back on her. "Listen, you'll figure it out, just like you've figured out everything in your life so far."

"I'm afraid to fail," he said. "I'm afraid to fail you, and I'm afraid to fail me, and I'm afraid to fail us."

He was a beautiful, beautiful man, and Penny smiled at the floor for some reason. "Right now, you're not failing me, or you, or us. So try to get some sleep tonight, and call me after church tomorrow. We'll go over your plan to wow Justin on Monday with your amazing ideas."

That got him to chuckle, and Penny was glad she could end the conversation on a more positive note.

"I sure do you like you, Penny Aarons," he said. "I'll talk to you tomorrow."

"Bye, Gideon." Penny turned and sighed as she walked over to the cradle and hung up the phone.

Her mother stood there, concern etched in every line of her face. "How's Gideon?"

"Amazing," Penny said, stepping into her mother's arms. "I like him so much, Mom." She pulled back and looked at her mother. "I'm falling in love with him. Is it crazy?"

"Of course not," her mother said. "He's a fine young man."

"I'm nineteen," Penny whispered, pressing her cheek to her mother's shoulder. "I have years to go before law school, and then years of that. What if...?"

"Sometimes plans change, Pen," her mom said gently. "There's no sense in worrying about what-if. Now go on and get to bed. You have to crate the five dozen packages in the morning, and I won't let you skip church." She stroked Penny's hair, a song starting in her chest. Penny stayed within the circle of her mother's arms as she hummed the childhood lullaby, and then she straightened.

"Love you, Mom."

"I love you too, Penny." She tucked her hair behind her ear, such love on her face. "You'll make the right decision with Gideon. You're smart, and so is he."

Penny nodded and moved around the corner and up the steps to her bedroom. Pure exhaustion filled her, and after she'd changed into her pajamas and brushed her teeth, she knelt beside her bed and begged the Lord to guide her when it came to Gideon.

Once under the covers, Penny closed her eyes and tried to go to sleep, but the words *family or career?* looped through her mind on repeat. She wanted both; she always had. The real question was would she be willing to give up Gideon to be a lawyer?

9

Gideon sat in his chair and listened to Justin talk about Intel's 4004 microprocessor. He could barely understand the concept, but Justin held the calculator in his hand.

"It's brand new," he said. "And they designed this chip as a central processing unit. It's incredible. It's going to change things." He didn't look happy about that, though Gideon bordered on thrilled.

"Word is that Texas Instruments is going to be releasing a new model in the fall too," Justin continued, stepping over to Gideon's desk and putting down the calculator. He continued to detail what the other companies were doing, and then he asked, "What can IBM do to compete?"

"I'm not sure why we even need to," Thomas said from Gideon's right. "Our line of office products isn't where

IBM makes its money." He glanced around at the other four men gathered in the conference room. "Right? What am I missing?"

"It's brand-new technology," Reid said. "That's what you're missing. It's about more than calculators."

"So you're saying we need a microprocessor too? We have thousands of clients around the world with the 370, and our software department can't keep up." Thomas frowned. "I'm not sure we're going to enter the market with a *calculator* that's going to drive us forward."

Gideon listened to them all talk. He listened to the ideas being offered, his mind whirring through how he could contribute.

In the next lull, he said, "IBM needs to consider the possibility of going small."

Justin turned toward him, and even Reid, the most senior product development engineer did as well. "What do you mean?"

"I mean," Gideon said slowly, his synapses firing now. "This is a microprocessor. It's small. People like small things. They like things that fit in their homes or the palm of their hand. Look at televisions—they're getting smaller and smaller as we find ways to improve the components."

He reached for the calculator. "Look at this model—it's fifteen percent smaller than the last one. Everything costs less when it's not as bulky." He turned to Thomas. "Thomas is right that IBM is leading the industry for business computers, but they're big, and bulky, and companies need entire rooms to house them. We dominate there, and no one's arguing that."

"Our corporate lawyers are actually trying to argue that," Justin said. "But I know what you're saying."

Gideon nodded, because yes, IBM had been accused of attempting to monopolize the market for business computing.

"What I'm trying to say is we shouldn't be trying to design our own microprocessor. We should be meeting with Intel to partner with them. We should be thinking beyond the calculator."

"To what?" Reid asked. "A personal computer?"

"Exactly," Gideon said, seeing a vision in his mind that had a computer in every home in America. "A personal computer. A small version of what we use here to run things. Men and women would use them for...personal things."

"What, exactly?" Justin challenged.

Gideon sat back, his brain buzzing. "Well, for one, the possibilities are endless. But for an example, take anyone who has to deal with finances to run their business. We do, and we have a machine to help us with the math, just like NASA does. On a personal level, my father could use a personal computer to keep his books. No more ledgers. No more paper receipts—and you pair this with the magnetic stripe technology IBM has, and you've offered ranchers and farmers across the country a faster, easier way to do their books."

Gideon looked around at everyone. "They do it right from their homes, on their personal computer."

"That's insane," Marcus said. "Can you imagine how much that would cost for a family? Farmers and ranchers can't afford that."

Gideon just looked at him. "The more advancements we have, the cheaper it will all be to produce."

Justin sat down, a thoughtful look on his face.

"The corner store owner could use the machine for transactions," Gideon offered. "We offer retail establishments the stripe capability, and they go from hand-writing receipts and counting money at the end of every day to printing a record and having the computer keep track of the math for them."

"You're talking about a simple adding machine," Reid said. "That's exactly what we already have. Adding machines. Calculators. This is office product talk."

"Sure," Gideon said. "But it's not an adding machine. It's a computer. It doesn't just spit out a number at the end. It's a complex system that we can program to do whatever we want. Not only that," Gideon said, about to reveal his real passion. "But IBM is going to need a whole new department for the security of these computers. Systems can be hacked—we saw that with AT&T and John Draper. We'd be absolutely blind if we didn't start thinking about and developing security for our machines."

Gideon's excitement leveled up. "Remember the MIT

students?" Reid and Thomas simply looked at him blankly.

"Yes," Justin said. "The UNIX thing."

"Right," Marcus said. "They rewrote the code, and it was actually better than what they started with."

"They're hacking systems," Gideon said. "The phone lines are just systems. Computers are just systems. And we're going to need a department dedicated to preventing that on our machines. Our customers will buy it, because they want their system to be safe." He looked around at everyone. "So we shouldn't be thinking office products or sending a memo to Development. We should be thinking *bigger*—by thinking *small*. IBM is poised here, gentlemen, to take computers to the masses."

The silence in the room filled him with joy, and Gideon couldn't wait to get home that night and call Penny.

He waited for the protests to come, but no one said anything. Finally, Justin stood up and buttoned his suit coat. "Gideon, what do we do next?"

"We call Intel, and we start talking to them about the 4004. We should be thinking of *partnering* with them, not competing with them."

"At least in the beginning," Marcus said.

"Right," Reid said. "Then we can see what they're doing and get our engineers in the labs too."

"The market is wide open for this," Gideon said, almost to himself. "This is only the beginning."

"You're with me this week, Gideon," Justin said. "Let's meet tomorrow and see if we can get the chip out of this calculator." He turned toward Reid. "Who do we know at Intel? Will they talk to us?"

"I'll call my guy," Reid said, standing up. "I have another meeting."

"Me too," Justin said. "Nine tomorrow, Gideon?"

"I'll be there." He stood with the others and left the conference room. Instead of going back to his desk, he went all the way downstairs and outside, unable to be contained by walls right now. His happiness morphed to joy and excitement, and he paused by the fountain in the courtyard and closed his eyes.

Thank you, thank you, thank you, he thought, praising the Lord for his good performance in his meeting today.

"That sounds terrible," Gideon said, smiling despite Penny's story about the sprinkler that had broken, causing a muddy, filthy mess in one of their free-range hen fields.

"I was covered," Penny said. "I think I still have some mud under my nails." She didn't sound happy about it either. She sighed while he chuckled. "What are you doing tomorrow?" she asked, changing the subject. "I bet you can guess what I'll be doing."

He loved her dry, sarcastic tone, and he looked up from the two dogs at his feet. The front yard at the ranch stretched before him, and it took every ounce of willpower he had not to get behind the wheel of his truck again and go see her right now.

Darkness had already started to fall though, and he'd only get an hour with her at the most.

Not only that, but he'd planned a surprise visit in the morning, and he didn't want to ruin that.

"I don't know," he said, and at least that was the truth. "Probably go to the park or something. Rent a canoe."

"That sounds fun," she said. "I'm going to...wait for it... crate eggs!" She laughed afterward, but Gideon got the feeling she was ready to be done in the egg warehouse.

He laughed with her and reached down to pat Moose. "I've got to get to the bookstore and get my books too," he said.

"Wait," she said. "I thought we were going to do that together when I get there next weekend."

Gideon's grin could've lit the entire state of Texas. "Oh, right, I forgot about that."

"So don't go without me," she said. "I'm making my father leave here at eight-thirty on Saturday morning," she said. "I'll get unpacked, and I'll meet you for lunch."

"I can't wait,' he said, his voice sticking in his throat.

"Me either," she said. "Only eight more days."

Gideon hoped they'd always count down the days until they could see one another again. "I should go," he said. "It's getting late, and it's been a busy week for me."

"It sure has, Mister Big Shot at IBM."

Gideon laughed again, shaking his head. "I'm not a big shot." He had been to plenty of conferences with the upper level management at IBM that week, and he, Reid, and Justin had started talking to Intel. "But I sure do like you, Penny Aarons."

"I sure do like you too, Gideon Walker," she said, and the call ended.

He lowered the phone from his ear, glad his mother had put one on the front table by the front door. He looked at it, thinking it sure would be nice if this thing didn't have a cord. Then he could take it anywhere he wanted. His mind started to whir again, but he got up and put the phone back in the cradle.

"Gideon, do you have a second?"

He turned at the sound of his father's voice, a tremor of trepidation tripping through him. "Sure, Dad," he said. He followed his dad back into the kitchen, where his mother sat at the dining room table, a cup of steaming tea in front of her. How she drank that in the height of the Texas summer, Gideon would never understand.

His father sat at the table too, and when Gideon spotted the envelope there, his stomach started to riot. "What's going on?" he asked. Neither hide nor hair of Jonas or Spencer could be found, and Gideon sensed an intervention of sorts.

"Nothing," his dad said. "Sit down."

Gideon sat, looking from his father to his mother. He

waited, his throat tightening with every second that passed.

"First, we want to apologize for not having a conversation with you about the ranch," Daddy started.

"Dad," Gideon said, frustration behind the single word. "It's fine. We don't need to keep going over this."

"Gideon," his mother said. "Just listen."

He nodded and looked down at the table. He really hadn't meant to make his father feel bad. At the same time, he should've had a conversation with all three of his sons about the ranch, Spencer included.

"We know it's not the same," Daddy said. "But we wanted to give you this as you're now going off into the world on your own." He pushed the envelope toward Gideon, who picked it up and opened it.

Money sat inside. Hundred dollar bills. A lot of them. Surprise and horror struck him right behind his lungs. "I don't need this." He set it down and slid it back to his dad. "I have a good job at IBM, Daddy. I'm doing great."

"We want you to have it," Momma said. "Because we love you, and you're our son." She looked at him with such earnestness in her expression that he couldn't argue with her. "If you don't need it now, save it. Then you'll have something to fall back on when times are lean."

Gideon nodded as his father passed him the envelope again.

"Things are serious with Penny, aren't they?" his mother asked.

Gideon yanked his gaze back to hers. "I suppose," he said.

"I see how you are with her," Momma said. "I'd say they're serious, or about to be. Use that to buy her a nice ring."

Heat filled Gideon's face. "You don't think it's too fast?"

"Heaven only knows that," Momma said. "I met your father in the—"

"Grocery store," Gideon said with a smile. "I've heard this story a thousand times, Momma."

She smiled fondly at Daddy, and Gideon could see their love as plainly as the sun shone. He'd always felt it between them too, and he wondered if he looked at Penny like that. His chest warmed in the same way, and he suspected he was very, very close to being in love with her.

It all felt crazy, but, "You were married in under three months," he said. "Love at first sight."

"Something like that," Daddy said gruffly as he got up from the table. "It's late, and we're moving cattle tomorrow."

Gideon scrambled to his feet, the envelope clutched in his hands. "Love you, Daddy."

"Love you too, son," he said as he hugged Gideon. His father didn't show emotion or get too physical, so the words and the embrace were real and important to Gideon.

His mother repeated them, and they left him alone in the kitchen.

He looked into the envelope again, thinking of the beautiful diamond the money could buy for Penny. A smile filled him from top to bottom, and he couldn't wait to see her tomorrow.

———

Gideon pulled up to the egg warehouse the next morning, the white paper pastry bag his only passenger. Mack and Moose had somehow known he was going to see Penny, and they'd wanted to come. Maybe it was the way he'd talked about her non-stop that morning as he mowed the front lawn for her father.

He didn't want to show up too early, but he didn't want to miss her either. It was just after eight now, and Gideon's nerves pranced through his whole body. What if he was too early? Acting too eager?

"Just go," he told himself. Calling her every night was definitely eager, and he did that.

He collected the pastry bag from the front seat and got out of his truck. The air was already hot, but it was quiet and peaceful here at the egg farm. Gideon liked this place; Penny was right. It did have a calm, relaxing feel to it.

He walked over to the door and reached for the knob. He hoped she'd be surprised, and that he could spend the day with her. By not telling her he was coming, she might've made other plans.

Gideon stepped inside, noticing first that it wasn't any cooler in here than outside. The noise level went up, because there were two huge fans blowing toward a long, stainless steel table in the shape of an L.

Penny stood in the nook of the L, right in front of a conveyor belt, lifting three eggs in each hand off the belt at a time.

She was stunning, though her hair had wisps falling out of its ponytail and she wore a T-shirt with the picture of a duck on it.

His face burst into a smile as she looked over to the door, the light from outside probably catching her attention.

She froze, her eyes wide. Gideon started laughing, and he suddenly couldn't get to her fast enough.

"Hey, love," he said as he crossed the space between them.

She dropped the eggs back onto the conveyor belt and hurried around the table to greet him. "Gideon." She ran her hands up the side of his face, tipped up onto her toes, and kissed him.

It was the best welcome Gideon had ever gotten.

10

"I can't believe it," Penny said again, looking up at him. "You're here." She kept moving her fingers up the back of his neck and into his hair, as if trying to convince herself that he was real.

"Surprise," he whispered, touching his lips to her jaw. "I brought breakfast too."

"Oh, now you're just showing off," Penny teased. She'd been in a terrible mood that morning, because she didn't want to spend another weekend alone. She'd wanted to drive to Austin to see Gideon, and her father had said no. She wasn't all that experienced with driving, that was true. But Austin was only an hour away, and it seemed silly to pine for Gideon at home when she could see him in an hour.

And now, here he was.

"At least I thought I brought breakfast," he said,

pulling away. "I had a pastry bag in my hand, I swear." He searched the floor, and sure enough, he stooped to pick it up. He grinned at her as he opened the bag. "Raspberry fritter for the pretty girl." He handed it to her, and she almost burst into tears.

He was so good. So kind, and thoughtful, and amazing.

She took the fritter and bit into it, the sweetness of the glaze combining with the tartness of the raspberry in the dough. "Mm." Her eyes rolled back in her head as he laughed.

"Wow, I've missed you," he said next, his hand brushing the side of her face as he tucked her hair behind her ear. He was tall, tough, and pure male, but his touch was gentle and soft.

She looked at him, the need to kiss him again almost debilitating. She did just that, only pulling away when the speaker system from the back of the warehouse crackled. Darren's voice came through with, "Pen? What's going on out there? We're backing up in here."

"Oh, my goodness," Penny said, her heartbeat jumping into the back of her throat. "The eggs." She handed the fritter back to Gideon and ran around the table to the conveyor belt.

Luckily, she'd just laid out three of the five-dozen crates, and she started picking up the eggs as quickly as she could.

"I can help," Gideon said as he set the pastry bag on

the corner of the table and rounded it to stand on the other side of the belt. "Doesn't look too hard."

"Get it done, then, cowboy," she said, her smile lifting her mouth in almost a clownish way.

He was here. She couldn't believe he was *here*.

The door behind her opened, and Darren said, "We're backing up."

"I know," Penny said over her shoulder. "I'm getting caught up."

"What—?" Darren paused as he joined her at the belt. He reached for the eggs with one hand, and he only picked up one. "Hello, Gideon."

"It's my fault," Gideon said. He at least picked up two eggs at a time, and he was using both hands. "I distracted her for a minute."

"I bet you did."

Penny elbowed her older brother in the ribs. "We're fine. Look. We're almost caught up already."

"All right, all right," Darren said. "I was just wondering. You don't normally fall behind."

"Didn't lose a single egg," Penny said as he started back toward the door. He left, and Penny looked at Gideon. He'd found his cowboy hat on the floor too, and he'd repositioned it on his head. "Did you drive down this morning?"

"Last night," he said.

"Last night?" Penny stared at him. "Gideon Walker,

are you telling me that you called me from your parents' house last night?"

"Yes, ma'am." He kept his head down, that brim a maddening barrier between the two of them.

She huffed, because she'd literally sat home alone last night. Her parents had gone to visit her aunt, and all three of her brothers had dates.

"I wanted it to be a surprise, sweetheart," he said.

"I would've been just as surprised last night as I was this morning."

"Yeah, but then I wouldn't have gotten to see you in action." He finally lifted his eyes to hers, and oh, he knew he was gorgeous and charming. The sparkle in his dark eyes said it all. "I wanted to see the egg warehouse. You've never showed it to me."

"That's because it's not anything to be excited about," she said. "Though, did you see the big rigs when you pulled in? We just got them back from the detail shop, and they have tiger teeth on the front." She did like those, and the paint job brought her an unreasonable amount of joy.

"I didn't see them," he said. "I was a little nervous and pretty focused on just getting myself through the door."

"Why were you nervous?"

He looked at her. "Because you're you."

She smiled at him. "Is that a compliment, Mister Walker?"

"Yes," he said, picking up another couple of eggs. "I

can't wait until you're in Austin. I can meet you at your apartment to unpack."

"That would be great," she said. "My dad is kind of pitching a fit about being gone, but he won't let me drive myself."

"I'll meet you, and he can go as soon as the last box is out of the truck."

Penny smiled and said, "I'm sure you'll earn some extra points for that."

Gideon put his eggs in the crate, and Penny deftly stacked the three she'd laid out, one right on top of the other. She pushed the stack in line with the others, stretching way across the table to do it, and reached for three more crates.

"Do I need points?" Gideon asked.

Penny looked at him while she picked up the eggs. She'd been doing it so long, she didn't even need to see them. "I don't think so."

"I was hoping you and I...." He cleared his throat. "I'm not sure what your plans are for today, but I was thinking we could go to Jenner's."

A squeak came out of Penny's mouth. "Gideon?"

"It's not a proposal," he said quickly. "But a man would like to know what his girlfriend likes in a diamond, so that if and when he's ready to make that step, he can get her a ring she'll like."

Penny stopped picking up eggs, but Gideon kept going. "Gideon," she said again.

His chest rose and then fell, and then he looked at her. "I'm about five minutes away from being in love with you," he said, just like that. "Maybe you're not there yet. Maybe you won't get there. I'm not saying we're going to get married next week, or even engaged anytime soon. I'm just...."

He looked down again, working to get the eggs in the crate. Penny couldn't move, and she wasn't sure why.

Five minutes? He was only five minutes away from being in love with her?

"I just thought it would be fun," he said. "If you don't want to go—"

"I do," she said.

He yanked his gaze to hers, and she realized what she'd said.

She clapped one hand over her mouth and shook her head. "I didn't mean—I don't mean I do-I do. I just—I'd like to go to Jenner's with you."

"Okay, then."

"Okay." Penny managed to pick up an egg and put it in the tray. She felt like she'd never done it before, and her heart raced in circles in her chest. "What else were you thinking sounded like fun?"

"Lunch," he said. "And then, well, I haven't thought much farther than the jewelry store and lunch."

"They're doing the hot air balloons at Stinger's Ranch," she said. "Darren mentioned that he was going with his girlfriend."

"Sure," Gideon said. "Whatever you want, Pen."

Penny felt like someone had stuck a light bulb inside her, and the glow of it was spreading through her whole body.

Whatever she wanted.

She wanted Gideon, she knew that.

She wanted a family.

She wanted to be a lawyer.

Those three things still didn't line up in her mind, but she told herself what Gideon had just told her. *It's not like you're going to get married next week—or even engaged.*

She had time to figure things out. Today, she just wanted to enjoy the time with her boyfriend.

———

"Right here, Daddy," Penny said. "See where that blue car came out of?"

"I see it," her dad said, and he turned into the small parking lot. Her building was off the main road, behind a couple of other apartment buildings, and Penny liked that. It meant there wouldn't be a lot of traffic, and no noise.

Her dad backed into a parking space close to the steps, and the two of them got out of the truck. She glanced around for Gideon, because he'd said he'd be there to help. She didn't see him, and she waited at the tailgate for her father to lower it.

"I'm on the third floor," she said.

"Of course you are," her dad grumbled as he picked up two boxes.

Penny frowned, but she didn't say anything. Brandon had offered to bring her to Austin, but her father had insisted he do it. She'd helped every step of the way, and she'd had everything packed and ready.

Yes, it was time out of his day, and Penny regretted that. But then he should've let Brandon bring her.

She followed him up the three flights of stairs to the top floor of the apartment building and turned left. The front door was open, and it was clear some of her roommates had already moved in.

Hannah poked her head out of the kitchen and said, "Penny."

Penny squealed and dropped her purse and backpack to hug Hannah. They laughed together, and suddenly it wasn't so bad that her dad was in a grumpy mood.

"I left you tons of room for the sewing machine," Hannah said as she pulled away. "And I've got coffee on if you or your dad wants some."

Her dad had taken her boxes into her bedroom, and she glanced at him as he returned. "Hannah, my dad. Daddy, you remember Hannah, right? We roomed together last year."

"Yes, of course."

Penny almost rolled her eyes at the kindness in her father's tone. "She said she has coffee. You want some?"

"Not right now," he said, glancing at her. "Let's just

get unloaded." With that, he left the apartment again, and Penny stooped to pick up her stuff.

"Thanks, Hannah," she said, hurrying to put her purse and bag on her bed. Twenty minutes later, and with Hannah's help, Penny had everything she needed on the third floor and not in the truck.

"All right, sugar bean," Daddy said, pulling Penny into a tight hug. "You be safe, and you be good, and you work hard."

"I will, Daddy," she said.

"I love you." The words came out almost choked, and Penny realized then why he wanted to drive her. He loved her. He wanted to bring her to college, though it was very hard for him to do that.

"Love you, too, Daddy."

He stepped back and nodded. "Call your mother tonight, okay, baby?"

"I will," Penny said.

He got behind the wheel of the truck and drove away, leaving Penny in the parking lot, with three flights of stairs to climb, a sewing machine to set up, a bed to make, and boxes to unpack.

She watched the truck until it turned and she couldn't see it anymore.

"Where in the world is Gideon?" she wondered, because he was really late, and Gideon was hardly ever late.

She didn't see him, and she had work to do, so she climbed the steps and got to it.

An hour later, someone knocked on the apartment door. The three girls who'd moved in already looked at one another. "That sounded kind of aggressive," Hannah said. She got up from the couch and peered through the slats in the blinds. "I can't see the front door from here. I don't know what I'm doing."

"I'll just get it," Penny said, as she was the closest. She got up and ran her hands through her hair quickly, then stepped over to the door and opened it.

Gideon stood there, his head down. He lifted his eyes to hers, and he wore remorse and regret there.

"Gideon," she said, wishing her chest wasn't quite so tight.

"Hi, sweetheart."

"Oh, you don't get to *sweetheart* me," she said. "You didn't show up to help, and you said you would." She gestured for him to come in. "My roommates were just taking bets on if you were real or not."

Gideon took off his cowboy hat as he stepped into the apartment.

"Here he is, girls," Penny said. "My boyfriend, Gideon Walker." She indicated the two other women standing in the living room. "Hannah's my roommate. Giselle lives across the hall from us. Our other roommate isn't here yet."

"Hello, ladies," Gideon said, worrying the brim of his

cowboy hat. He turned to Penny and didn't bother keeping his voice down when he said, "I had to go into work. I'm so sorry. I wanted to be here, but I had no way to call. I even called your mother, but she didn't have this number."

"You had to work on a Saturday?"

"We're really onto something right now," he said. "Justin called me about ten minutes before I would've left to come help. I swear. I'm sorry, Pen."

"How sorry?" Hannah asked, inserting herself into the conversation.

Gideon looked at her, clear confusion in his expression.

Penny understood where this was going though. "Yeah," she said, joining Hannah. The two of them folded their arms simultaneously. "How sorry? Like, sorry enough to go get doughnuts from The Flying Pig?" She looked at Hannah, and so much was communicated between them. "That would mean he's pretty sorry. I might just have to forgive him if he brought back the maple porker."

"Oh, no," Hannah said, with plenty of mock disgust in her voice. "If he wants to be forgiven, he's going to need to bring back the Elvis Presley."

They looked at Gideon, and Penny couldn't help the wide smile as it spread across her face.

He simply stared at her, as if she'd hit him upside the head with a two-by-four. "The Flying Pig?" he asked.

"It's a doughnut truck," Penny said. "My favorite. And

it's my first day in town, and my boyfriend was super late, and I'm starving, because he said he'd bring breakfast, and look. No breakfast."

Gideon's smile took longer to appear. "The Flying Pig. Maple porker. Elvis Presley." He turned to Giselle. "What do I need to do to earn your forgiveness?"

Giselle, who Penny didn't know hardly at all, looked from him to Penny and back. "Do you have a brother?"

Penny burst out laughing, and she linked her arm through Gideon's. "Come on, cowboy," she said. "I'll go with you to get the doughnuts."

11

Gideon swiped the stack of folders from his desk without breaking his stride. He was late leaving for class. He'd been late to his meeting this morning too, because his brainstorming session with Justin had gone over.

Gideon hated being late, but he felt like he'd been running behind for a week now.

School had started, and while Justin had originally given him permission to leave at 2 p.m. on Tuesdays and Thursdays, he was two days in and it wasn't going well.

He had homework already, and he'd stayed late at work on Monday and Wednesday to keep caught up with his responsibilities.

He barely had time to eat, shower, and sleep, and he hadn't seen Penny in days. He'd called her a couple of times, but that had really been to reschedule their date.

A frown pulled through him and across his face, because he had a feeling he'd have to cancel tomorrow too.

It was always busy at the beginning of a new semester, Gideon knew. Things would settle down once he figured out how to balance everything.

He loved his job at IBM, and he was learning so much there. His classes focused on patent law, technology advancements, and business administration systems.

Gideon felt like he needed the classes, but his on-site experience was valuable too. He and Justin were still in negotiations with Intel, but they hadn't slammed the door in their faces.

Meanwhile, the higher-ups at IBM had given the development department the charge to "figure out" the microprocessing chip.

As if it were that easy.

Gideon hurried to his truck and he may have driven a bit over the speed limit to get to campus. He slipped in the back of the classroom and glanced around for a place to sit. Thankfully, this was the second day of class, and humans were creatures of habit. They stuck to where they'd sat on the first day, and Gideon managed to go down a couple of rows and step over one person to get to a seat. He took a notebook out of his backpack and tried to clue in to what the professor was saying.

His mind drifted, because he was tired, and he had a ton of other things to do. Frustration built in him over the next few hours, because he felt like he was wasting his time.

By the time he got home, pure exhaustion pulled through him. He managed to make scrambled eggs and toast, and he ate at the small table in the kitchen with his folders in front of him.

The next thing he knew, the telephone woke him. Its shrill ring startled him, and he sat up straight, his heart pounding.

The room had gotten darker, but it wasn't all the way dark yet.

He jumped to his feet as his full awareness came back, and he quickly crossed the kitchen to the phone.

"Hello?"

"Gideon," Penny said.

A smile touched his lips. "Hey, sweetheart."

"You forgot, didn't you?"

Gideon's synapses started firing, because the disappointment in her voice combined with her words had surprised him. "I suppose I did." Because he still couldn't remember what he'd forgotten.

"It's okay," she said. "Hannah can borrow her boyfriend's car. We can use that to go grocery shopping."

"Oh, the grocery shopping," he said, foolishness moving through him. "I'm sorry. I can come right now."

"It's okay," Penny said, but Gideon had the feeling it wasn't.

"I'll leave right now," he said. "I'll be there in ten minutes."

Penny didn't protest again, but she did sigh.

Gideon reached for his keys, because he wanted to see Penny. "Ten minutes," he said again, and he hung up and headed out.

He'd gotten a little nap at the table, and by the time he got to Penny's apartment, he was wide awake. She waited on the bottom step of the staircase that led up to her apartment.

Gideon put the truck in park, left it running, and got out. Penny stood, and she was the best thing he'd seen in days. "I'm so sorry." He took her into his arms, and he was glad she let him. The storm she wore on her face hadn't been hard to see.

"I'm just busy right now," he said, his mouth at her ear. "I'll get a schedule worked out, I swear."

"It's fine," she said. "Hannah had already called her boyfriend, so it's just me." She stepped back and straightened her blouse. She wore a pink, purple, and red striped shirt with a dark brown pair of corduroy pants, and Gideon wondered if she'd made them. She made a lot of her clothes, and they fit like a glove.

He reached for her hand. "I'm sorry," he said again.

A smile finally appeared on her face, and he felt like she'd started to forgive him. "How's class?" she asked.

"Uh, long," Gideon said. "I think I'm going to need to drop one of them."

"Which one?"

"Patent law," he said. "There's no way I can keep up with the homework and keep my job." And Penny.

He glanced at her, and she nodded. "If you think you should."

"I should," he said. "I'll call them tomorrow." He opened the passenger door for her, and Penny paused instead of getting in.

"I miss you, Gideon." She stretched up and kissed him, and Gideon knew he couldn't neglect her, or he'd lose her. He couldn't forget the things he said he'd do for her, and as he kissed her, he vowed to do better.

After she pulled away, he said, "I'll do better, okay?"

"The beginning of the semester is busy," she said. She climbed into the truck, and Gideon went around to the driver's side.

"How have your classes been?" he asked, glancing at her. "Good? Hard?"

"Two of them won't be too bad," she said. "It's advanced chemistry that's going to take most of my time." She looked out her window, and she was simply beautiful to him. She'd braided her auburn hair that day, and he liked the way she sat with her purse in her lap.

He enjoyed walking around the grocery store with her. Such a simple thing, but so much fun. She opened up more once there, and by the time he dropped her off, things between them were back to normal.

Gideon made it home, a sigh coming out of his mouth

as he got out of the truck and went inside. "It's just the beginning of the semester," he told himself as he left the folders on the table and went down the hall to his bedroom.

He brushed his teeth and changed into his pajamas and dropped to his knees. "Lord," he said. "I know I need to do better. I just don't know how."

He fell silent, because that was the gist of everything streaming through him. Maybe he just didn't have enough time to do everything. He wanted the job at IBM for sure. He needed a way to make money.

He wanted Penny too, and a man needed to be able to support his wife and family.

As he got in bed, he looked up at the ceiling. "Maybe I should drop the classes."

If he wanted to keep Penny and keep his job, he probably should.

He'd sleep on it, and then he'd decide when he wasn't so tired, and so overwhelmed, and fresh off a failure with his girlfriend.

12

Penny looked up as the bus started to slow again. She still had four stops to go, and she could probably get through this next section in her chemistry book. She had a test coming up, and she wanted to score the highest.

The professor put up a list of the scores, with numbers as the identifier for each person. On the last test, she'd been second. The competitive spirit inside her wanted that top spot, especially since the person who'd been at the top had bragged about it to everyone on campus.

Okay, that was an exaggeration, but everyone in the class knew Trevor Seamons had scored the highest. He'd made sure of that.

He'd also made sure that Penny knew he was smarter than her. He sneered at her in the lab, and he scowled when she answered questions correctly.

She was fine with how he treated her. She was fine

studying on her own, though she'd heard several others making groups and talking about sharing notes.

They hadn't invited her, because the class was ninety-five percent men, and they didn't know what to do with Penny.

She looked up again, her eyes moving to the man standing at the back of the bus. He looked away, but Penny knew he'd been watching her. She went back to her book, but now she could feel his eyes.

She hadn't seen him before, but he did seem familiar. If he went to UT-Austin and rode this bus, she might have seen him before.

She gave up on the chemistry and stuck her book back in her pack. She stood up once her stop was next, and she stepped right past the man as she got off the bus.

He got off right after her. Penny's heartbeat accelerated, but she forced herself to walk at a normal speed and not look over her shoulder.

Maybe this was his stop too. The others who'd gotten off dispersed, and Penny started down the street toward the white apartment buildings a couple of blocks down.

She could hear footsteps behind her, but she refused to turn and look.

Gideon had promised to pick her up right after school today, because she'd told him she'd make dinner for them tonight. He was going to show her where he lived, and she was excited to spend the evening with him.

They hadn't seen each other much over the past

month, but Penny had barely settled into her own sched-ule, and she couldn't imagine working as much as Gideon did *and* going to school.

Gideon had dropped the patent law class, and he'd seemed to be able to manage his responsibilities better. But she missed him immensely. She'd thought things would be different once they were living in the same place, but she'd forgotten how busy college was.

She paused at the corner to wait for the light to change. The man who'd been watching her stepped up beside her. Their eyes met, and Penny's natural reaction was to smile. So she did.

He returned it, and Penny supposed he was good-look-ing. He had dark brown hair, and dark brown eyes, and a much darker complexion than she did. He wasn't as tall as Gideon, and he didn't have a cowboy hat, so that was defi-nitely a strike against him.

Not that Penny was looking for another boyfriend. In fact, nothing about this man called to her the way every-thing about Gideon did.

"Hey," he said.

"Hi."

Penny tightened the straps on her backpack and faced forward. She didn't want to encourage him, and she had a feeling she was going to have to reject him.

When the light turned green, they stepped off the curb together, and he said, "I'm Simon."

"Penny," she said, trying to keep her voice crisp.

"I was wondering if you ride that bus every night," he said.

"Yes," she said. "I live one street over." In fact, she could cross the street now and cut through a couple of parking lots to get to her building. Maybe she should. Then she could spare Simon's feelings and avoid an awkward situation.

"I'm in Cambridge Court," he said.

"Oh, I'm just across the street from that," she said. "King Henry Court."

"Right, I think I've seen you before." Simon smiled at her, and he wasn't nervous. They walked to the next corner and turned to go across the street.

Her building was on this side and his on the other, and as Penny approached, she had a feeling Simon was going to ask her out.

"I was wondering if you'd want to get together," he said. "For dinner or something." He paused next to the sidewalk that led to his building.

Penny took a couple more steps and turned back to him. "I can't, Simon. I'm sorry."

"Okay," he said. "Boyfriend?"

"Yes," she said. "How did you know?"

Simon nodded past her, and Penny turned to find Gideon walking down the sidewalk toward them. Her whole soul lit up, and she knew the difference between Simon and Gideon instantly.

"Hey, sweetheart," he said, his voice far too loud. He

put his arm around her, and Penny gaped at him. She'd never seen jealousy on him, and he wore it obviously.

"This is Simon," Penny said. "Simon, this is Gideon."

"Nice to meet you," Gideon said, his smile plastic as he reached to shake Simon's hand.

"You too," Simon said. "I was just going to ask Penny if she wanted to get together to study with me."

Penny whipped her attention back to him. His smile was much more relaxed. "I saw you with that chemistry book. I'm in that class with Monroe, and I'm pretty sure I'm going to fail."

"You want to study with me?" Penny asked, her hopes shooting higher than she'd thought they would. No one ever wanted to study with her—no men at least.

"I have a feeling you know what you're doing," he said. "So yes, definitely."

Penny looked at Gideon, her eyes wide. His smile relaxed, and he nodded at Simon. "You should, Pen. You've always wanted a study group."

"Yes," Penny said, the strangest urge to hug Simon coming over her. "Let's get together to study."

"Great," Simon said, shrugging off his backpack. "If this next exam is as tough as Monroe says it's going to be, I'm going to need all the help I can get" He dug in his bag. "Let me find a pen to get your number...." He did, and he scratched his out and ripped the sheet off to give it to her. "And yours?"

She gave it to him, and he nodded. "I'll call you later to set something up. Or maybe I'll see you on the bus again."

"Okay," Penny said. "I'll be home later tonight." Giddiness filled her as Simon walked away. She turned to Gideon and squealed as she jumped into his arms.

He laughed with her, and once they started toward her building, she exhaled. "A real study group, Gideon."

"That's great, Pen," he said, but the words sounded a little false.

Penny looked at him and squeezed his hand. "You're not jealous, are you?"

"That's one-hundred percent yes," he said.

Penny laughed, because it was a laughable idea. He really had no idea how he affected her, or how amazing he was.

"You don't need to be," she said.

"No?"

"Absolutely not," she said, wondering how bold to be. She'd always said what she'd thought and felt with Gideon, and she saw no need to change now. "I felt nothing when I looked at him. Then I turned around and saw you, and...wow."

They reached his truck, and he took her backpack from her to lift it over the tailgate. He faced her. "Wow?"

"Wow," she repeated. "You're...." She didn't know how to tell him what she felt when she looked at him. They'd been dating for over two months now, which Penny knew wasn't a terribly long time, but she'd never once been bored with Gideon. He always had a fascinating story to tell about IBM, and he asked her about her life, her classes, her worries, her dreams. He seemed genuinely interested in her, and he supported everything she wanted to do in her life.

Gideon simply waited for her to tell him what he was, and Penny couldn't find the words. She stepped back into his arms and wrapped her hands around the back of his neck. His hands on her waist were warm and they fit perfectly. She closed her eyes and enjoyed the moment as he leaned his forehead against hers.

"You're amazing," she whispered, feeling like they were the only two people on the planet in that moment. "When I see you, instant joy fills me. My stomach swoops, and I can't wait for you to kiss me. I want to be with you every day, and I want to spend all my free time with you."

There. That summed it up really well, in her opinion.

"Wow," Gideon whispered. "That is something, I guess."

Penny opened her eyes and pulled away enough to see his face. "And? What happens when you see me?"

Gideon searched her face, his expression full of seriousness. She saw a burning fire of desire too, and she felt it moving through her as well.

"When I see you, all I can think about is making you my wife," he said.

Surprise shot through Penny, and her eyebrows lifted. She didn't know what to say, though they'd already looked at rings in Sweet Creek. He'd just never said anything about marriage again.

"I want to be yours," he said. "And I want you to be mine, and I want everyone—including guys like Simon—to know you're taken." He ducked his head. "Sorry about the jealousy. I guess it just reared up, and I saw you walking with him, and I got out to come meet you."

"It's fine," she said. "Are we really talking about getting married?"

"It's been on my mind," Gideon said. "I know it's fast, and I don't mind going slow. Maybe next summer or something."

"Hey, you two," Hannah said, and Penny stepped out of Gideon's arms though she hadn't kissed him yet and she really wanted to.

"Hey, Hannah," Gideon said, walking toward Penny's door. "How's school?"

"Busy," Hannah said. "I'm working tonight, Pen. I'll come in quietly."

"Okay," Penny said. "I'm making dinner at Gideon's, but I should be home before you."

"Have fun," she said, and she got in Rob's car as he pulled up.

"Should we go?" Gideon asked, and Penny nodded as she slipped past him.

The drive to his place only took ten minutes, and he pulled up to the cutest little white house Penny had ever seen.

"Wow, Gideon," she said. "This is so much better than an apartment."

"It is," he agreed. "I did the roommate thing for a while, and this is better."

They got out, and Penny looked at the emerald green lawn. "Do you do the yard work?"

"Yes," he said. "They give me a reduced rent if I do." He looked right down the street. "I help a lady down the road a bit too. She's single with a couple of little kids. I need to get down there and see how she's doing."

Penny's heart warmed at his kindness and care of others, and just when she didn't think she could find him more attractive, it turned out she could.

"I got everything you said you needed," he said, leading her into the house. "Kitchen here. That table is as close to a dining room as you'll get." He went through a doorway, and she took a moment to take in the kitchen.

A long counter took up the back of the house, and it had everything in that one strip. Fridge in the corner. Coffeemaker on the counter next to that. Stove. More counter space. Sink. More counter space.

She followed him into the living room, which held two couches and a big, boxy television.

"I spread out a little," he said, gathering up papers and stuffing them into folders. "The table isn't big enough."

"You don't have to clean up," she said. "We can stay in the kitchen."

He stopped and looked at her, a hint of his nerves

there. "Two bedrooms off the kitchen," he said. "I use one for an office, but the chair in there isn't very comfortable."

Penny smiled at him and asked, "Would you go get my backpack? I forgot it, and I need to study while the casserole bakes."

"Sure thing, sweetheart."

He left through the front door to do that, and Penny got to work on the chicken and wild rice bake she'd promised him. They chatted in the kitchen, and he told her about a man at work named Marcus who'd gone on his first date with a woman that had been a complete disaster.

Penny laughed harder than she ever had, and she curled into Gideon's side as they sat on the couch together, both of them studying something important to them.

For her, it was chemistry, and the time with Gideon was the epitome of what she wanted in her life.

His phone rang, and he eased away from her to go answer it. She could hear his voice from the kitchen, but she focused on the complicated processes in her book.

A minute later, he entered the living room again, the jangle of his keys alerting her to the fact that something was about to happen.

"I have to run into work for a minute," he said.

"You do?"

"I left something there that I need for Justin," he said. "I'm just driving there and back. I'll be gone maybe forty minutes." He stepped closer and swept a kiss along her hairline. "I'm sorry. The food still has twenty-five minutes in the oven. You'll barely know I've been gone."

"Okay," she said, and he left. Penny sat in his quiet house, wondering why she'd said it was okay for him to go. She didn't want him to go; she wanted to sit beside him and be with him.

She sighed as she went back to her studying. She took the food out of the oven when the timer went off. She poured herself a glass of the sweet tea he had in his fridge and went back to studying.

She completed her mathematics homework and finished her tea, and Gideon still hadn't returned.

Dinner grew cold, and Penny's patience ran out. She reheated the oven and stuck the food back in.

When he'd been gone for twice as long as he'd said he would be, she packed up her books and served herself a plate of chicken and wild rice, and she ate alone.

She stood at his sink, washing her plate, when he finally walked in.

"Sorry," he said, but Penny only glared at him. She left the plate in the sink and bent to get her backpack.

"I'm ready to go," she said.

"Go? We haven't eaten."

"I did," she said. "You do realize how long you've been gone, right?"

Gideon sighed and ran his hand down his face. "Justin was in the office, and I couldn't leave."

"Yes, you can," Penny said. "You say, 'hey, sorry, but

my girlfriend took time out of her busy schedule to make dinner for me, and I can't stay.' Then you walk out."

"It's not that simple, Pen," he said, stepping around her and picking up the second plate she'd gotten out of the cupboard. He put a piece of chicken on it and plenty of wild rice.

She blinked, and her whole future flashed before her eyes. "Will you always pick work over me?" she asked. She should at least know with perfect clarity what she was getting into.

"Of course not," he said.

"What if Justin calls when we're about to sit down to dinner? Or when it's time to bathe our son? Or when we're leaving to visit our parents? Or—?"

"Okay," Gideon said, throwing her a dark look. "I get it."

"You can't just run off whenever he calls."

"He's my boss," Gideon said. "And I love this job, and I'm learning so much."

Penny nodded, because she knew all of that. Gideon had said it all before. "You have to have a line you won't cross."

"I have to keep my job too," he said. "Who do you think is going to pay for the house we live in? Or the water bill to bathe that son?" He cocked his eyebrows at her.

"Your family should come first."

He took his plate to the table and sighed as he sat down. "I don't want to fight about this," he said. "I'm trying, Penny. I have to have a job. You want as many children as the Good Lord will give you. They're not free."

"I know that," she said quietly.

"Do you?" he asked, looking over his shoulder to where she stood. His glare punched her in the chest. "You can give up being a lawyer to be a mother, if that's what you want to do. I can't just leave my career on the line, because then we'll end up living with my parents. Or yours."

He turned around again, and all of Penny's nerves vibrated.

A full minute passed, and Penny didn't know what to say or do. He was right, but she was too. She didn't want him to run off every night just because someone called.

She wanted to be more important than some things.

"Please come sit with me," he said quietly. He looked at her. "Please?"

Penny crossed the kitchen on wooden legs and sat down at the only other chair at the table. He kept his head down as he ate, and the tension between them felt like it might snap her bones clean in half.

"I'm sorry," he finally said. "Maybe I do need to draw a line somewhere, but Pen, I don't know where to do that."

"I understand," she said.

Gideon looked at her, and everything hard on his face softened. "I can't stand you being mad at me," he whispered, reaching out to cup her face. "But I don't know how to stop disappointing you."

"You don't disappoint me," she said, feeling ridiculous for demanding he put her and their fictitious children above everything else.

"Yes, I do," he said. "I want to do something with my life, Pen. I want to invent something. I want to be right on the cutting edge of technology. I'm sure there's a line, but I fear if I draw it now, I'll miss out on something I really want to do."

She nodded, her boldness and bravery suddenly on vacation. So she didn't say what was circling through her mind.

If he didn't draw the line now, maybe he would miss out on something he really wanted—her, and the possibility of a life with her and those children the Good Lord would give them.

13

Gideon pushed the lawn mower back and forth, getting the grass cut at his place, hopefully for the last time for a while. Autumn had finally arrived in Austin, and the grass wasn't nearly as vibrant as it had been when he'd moved in.

When he finished at his place, he walked the mower down the road to Savannah's, where he found her two little boys playing happily on the front driveway.

He waved to them, a smile etched on his face, and got to work getting her lawn cleaned up too. She came out onto the front porch as he finished up and said, "Thank you, Gideon."

"Sure thing," he called to her. "Everything else okay? Need anything?"

"We're okay," she said with a smile. "Thanks, though."

He waved and went home to shower. It was the weekend, and he'd determined he would not work a minute of it. He'd drawn the line.

He had no idea what he'd do if Justin called or if Gideon suddenly remembered he needed to have a brief ready for a meeting on Monday morning.

A couple of weeks had passed since the awkward and tense night with Penny where she'd made the most delicious dinner he'd eaten since moving to Austin.

He could make a few things, but he didn't want to spend time in the kitchen, so his breakfasts consisted of coffee and toast, and his dinners were something he could whip up in minutes. Pancakes, eggs, sandwiches.

He put in a load of laundry and made a grocery list. He showered and switched his clothes to the dryer. He went and got his groceries, and right when he'd said he'd bring lunch to Penny and Simon, he pulled into her parking lot and reached for the paper bags of hamburgers and fries he'd bought.

Gideon liked Simon well enough, but he didn't believe for a single second that the man really only wanted to be Penny's study buddy. Gideon had tried that tactic to spend time with the woman he liked too, and he'd seen the way Simon looked at Penny—even if she didn't.

Their test was on Monday, and Gideon actually hoped the study group would break up after that.

"Hey," he said when he found them sitting at the single table behind her building. At least she was smart enough not to invite him into her apartment. They studied on campus or at this table, and Gideon took a moment to kiss her hello.

They hadn't spoken of marriage again, nor had Gideon promised something he couldn't deliver. He'd stopped asking her out for weeknights, as he usually spent those doing homework or at the office, and he really couldn't stomach the thought of disappointing Penny.

They'd spoken on the phone several times, and he'd seen her last weekend too.

"Thanks for the food," Simon said, and Gideon just smiled at him. They ate while Penny quizzed Simon with the note cards they'd made. When he started doing the same for her, Gideon pulled out his own homework and finished it.

He hated sitting around doing nothing, and his first thought was to go into the office and read the development report from that week.

No, he told himself. He wasn't working this weekend.

He couldn't turn off his brain though, and he really did hate sitting around. "How much longer are you guys going to be?" he asked.

Penny looked at him with surprise in her eyes. "The test is on Monday."

"So a while," he said. "If so, I'll catch up with you tonight, okay?" He stood from the picnic table and bent down to kiss her. She was definitely distracted, and as he walked away, annoyance burned through him.

"So it's okay for her to focus on what's important to

her—at my expense—but I can't do the same?" He shook his head as he got behind the wheel of his truck, and then he set himself on the highway and just drove.

By the time his irritation and frustration had ebbed, he was only fifteen minutes away from the ranch, and he figured he might as well visit his parents for a few minutes.

He pulled off the highway and went past the Walker family gate. Under the shade of the trees, he parked the truck and peered at the house.

No one came out to greet him, but that wasn't that surprising. They were probably all working, even his mother.

A dog barked, and then Moose jumped up and put his front paws on Gideon's window. He laughed as he opened the door and Moose fell back. "Hey, buddy."

Moose barked a few more times as Gideon rubbed him down.

"Oh, you're dirty," Gideon said as he chuckled. He dusted his hands off and looked around for Mack. The other dog came running around the corner of the house, and Gideon laughed as he nearly fell on his face in his exuberance.

The barking dogs had alerted his mother to someone at the farmhouse, and she'd come out onto the porch. "Gideon, baby," she said in her thick accent. "What are you doin' here?"

"Just came to visit," he said. "What are y'all up to around here?"

"I'm making applesauce today," she said.

In that moment, Gideon smelled the cinnamon floating on the air. He wondered how he'd missed it before.

"I can help you peel," he said.

His mother laughed. "Oh, you must be bored."

Gideon didn't confirm it or deny it, but he climbed the steps and took his mother into a hug. He loved the fierceness with which his mother hugged him, and he held her for an extra few seconds.

"What's wrong, baby?" she asked as she drew back.

"Nothing," Gideon said, his smile trembling a little.

"How's work?"

"Good."

"Your classes?"

"Fine."

"Gideon," she said. "I get more than one-word answers." She turned to go into the house, and he followed her. She gave him a break as she walked into the kitchen, which looked like a bomb filled with apples and jars had gone off.

She checked a timer and turned back to him. "This will go off in six minutes. I get to listen to you talk for that time. Then you can be done."

"I've got nothing to say, Momma," he said, sitting down at the table.

"How's Penny?"

Gideon sighed and reached up to take his cowboy hat off.

"Ah, there it is," Momma said. "Get talking, Gideon, or I'll turn this timer up."

She wouldn't, and he knew it, because she was using that to time the jars in the pressure cooker right now.

"We're serious," Gideon said. "I'm fairly sure I'm in love with her. I want to be with her. I want to build a family together. But, I also want this career at IBM. Or somewhere. Doesn't have to be IBM, but I'm learning a lot there. The possibilities are honestly endless, Momma. And I want to be in on all of them."

"I know you do, son."

"Penny wants me to pick her first," he said. "I want that too, but don't I have to make a living? I don't know how to balance those. How did you and Daddy do it?"

Momma reached over and covered Gideon's hands with hers. "It takes work. And forgiveness. And a lot of discussion. If you and Penny are serious about your relationship, you'll make time for each other. If she's serious about supporting you, and you're serious about supporting her, you'll figure out what that looks like for both of yous and what you can sacrifice and what you can't."

Gideon nodded, remaining quiet. His worries didn't ease much, though he had seen his mother and father work through things together.

The real issue was Penny. He needed to know what she was willing to put up with and what she wasn't. In the conversations they'd already had, it sounded like she wasn't willing to have him work past five p.m. or ever take phone calls at home.

To him, that was unreasonable, especially for his line of work.

"A conversation," he said. "I can do that." He didn't really want to, but Gideon had endured hard conversations in the past—most recently with his father and Jonas about the ranch.

He could talk to Penny too.

"Thanks, Momma." He stood up, thinking he'd just head back to Austin now. Penny would finish up her studying, and perhaps Gideon could call her and ask her to dinner. At the same time, he thought maybe he'd just head back to his little house, do some cleaning, and go look at dogs at the animal shelter.

He knew he couldn't get a pet right now, but he could look.

"You're leaving?" Momma asked. "Don't go. I can put on a fresh pot of coffee and whip up a pot of macaroni."

His mother's solution to most problems was macaroni and cheese. Gideon had never minded before, because his momma's cooking did soothe the soul. Her recipe had been handed down for generations, and Gideon loved the heritage of his ancestors.

"I can't stay long, Momma," he said. "I have to get back by five."

She glanced at the clock. "That's two hours, son." She stood up. "I'll get the water boilin'."

14

Penny pushed her notes across the table to Simon, ignoring the laughter coming from a group of students at the table behind them. "It's the electron isotopes Doctor Monroe was talking about in the last class."

Simon looked at the notebook, a blank expression on his face. "I was here for that, but my notes don't look like that at all." He sighed and put his head down. "I'm never going to get this."

"Sure you will," Penny said encouragingly. "You passed the last test."

"Barely," he said. "I wasn't anywhere near the top. That one person got ninety-nine percent." He sounded miserable, and Penny buried her nose in the book.

She was "that one person" who'd scored the highest on their last test. She hadn't told anyone in the class, and when she'd seen her number at the top—above Trevor's—she'd known no such joy.

She'd only told Gideon, and he'd laughed with her, spun her around, and kissed her after he'd told her how amazing she was.

He'd been mostly on time in the past couple of weeks, and they had plans for Halloween night. Both of them would take the whole night off—her from studying and him from his homework and work—and attend a costume party together.

Gideon didn't want to go at all. He'd rather stay home in his cowboy hat and hand out candy to the little children that came by his house. Penny had talked him into the campus-wide event, and she'd been praying it would be a success for the past week.

"Here comes trouble," Simon said under his breath, and Penny looked up. Simon kept his attention on her notebook, and she glanced to her right.

Trevor and his posse were only steps away. "What do we have here?" the man sneered.

Penny's defenses flew into place. She wanted to snap her notebook closed so he couldn't see anything he might have missed in class. "We're studying," Penny said, her voice hard.

Trevor grinned at the three other men with him. "The two losers of the class," he said. "It's cute how you think if you study, you'll actually pass."

"I did pass," Simon said.

Trevor put both hands on their table and leaned into them. "Probably at the very bottom of the cut."

"It doesn't matter," Penny said, her protective streak rising up as she stood. "He passed. It doesn't matter where." There'd been at least half a dozen scores lower than Simon's.

"Yeah? And where did you end up?" Trevor asked, his gaze sliding down Penny's torso.

She wanted to deck him right in the mouth. "None of your business." She didn't dare look back at her book though.

Trevor and his friends laughed, which only spurred Penny's anger. She coached herself not to respond. They didn't get to know her score. That was the point of using the student numbers, though a lot of people in the class simply told one another.

"Do you want to study with us?" Penny asked. "Maybe then you'll pass the next test too."

Trevor's laugh turned cruel, and Penny braced herself for an insult. "Please. I don't need you to help me pass." He knocked on the table. "I'll let you get back to it. I'm going to be applying to law school in the spring too, and you'll be up against me."

"I think Penny can handle you," another man said, and Penny's heart raced.

Gideon stood behind the other group, a couple of brown bags in his hand. He looked past Trevor to Penny, a smile coming over his face. "Hey, love."

She smiled back at him, because he was there. On time, with lunch, and defensive of her.

He stepped past Trevor while he and the others stared, and leaned down to kiss Penny. Before he did, he whispered, "Please let me tell them."

"No," she said, touching her lips to his real quick. "Thanks for bringing lunch." She took the bags and passed one to Simon.

"Thanks, Gideon," he said.

"Oh, the organic unit," Gideon said, his voice much too casual to actually be casual. "I didn't do well on this at all."

"Your girlfriend won't either," Trevor said. "It's really cute how she thinks she can be a lawyer."

Penny felt the indignation flow from Gideon. He took a step toward Trevor, who actually fell back.

"Here we go," Simon said, and he looked absolutely gleeful.

"She *can* be a lawyer," Gideon said. "Why wouldn't she be able to?"

"How many female lawyers do you know?" Trevor challenged.

"How is that relevant at all?" Gideon asked. "If she has the grades, she can apply and get in. She'll be ten times the lawyer you'll be." He looked down to Trevor's feet and back.

"Gideon, let it go," Penny said, though she fell a little more in love with him for what he'd said. He'd never made her feel like her dreams and ambitions were limited by her gender. He'd never made her feel like she wasn't smart enough to do whatsoever she wanted to do.

Gideon turned around. "I'm going to tell him."

Penny drew in a breath and gestured for him to get on with it then.

"She scored the ninety-nine on the last test," Gideon said, after zeroing in on Trevor and his group again. "I think you were what? Eighty-eight? Fourth in the class this time, I believe." He moved to Penny's side, their eyes meeting for the briefest moment. He put his arm around her, and they faced Trevor together.

"*You* got the ninety-nine?" Simon asked, his voice incredulous.

"Yes," Penny said.

"No way," Trevor said, his normal bluster completely gone.

"Seven-four-two-oh-two," Penny said. "That's me." She looked up at Gideon, who was smiling at Trevor as if to say, *So there.*

"Come on, baby," she said to Gideon. "Let's eat, and then you better get back to work."

"Sure thing, sugar." He laid the accent on extra thick, and Penny didn't mind a bit. "I got those sweet potato fries you like so much. The maple glaze is for you, Simon."

"Thanks, Gideon," Simon said. He fixed his gaze on Penny. "How in the world did you get ninety-nine?"

She just smiled at him and said, "Let's go over the respiration process again. I'm not so sure on that part."

Gideon took out her chicken salad and a bag of sweet potato fries while Trevor and his friends grumbled and walked away.

She sat back down, Gideon at her side, and she glanced at him as she put her hand on his leg under the table.

He met her eyes, and so much was said between them in that moment that Penny couldn't wait to be alone with him so she could kiss him with all the feelings currently running through her body.

"Respiration I get," Simon said, focusing on her notebook. "It's this reverse-osmo-something-or-other I don't understand."

———

A few days later, Penny swiped on the last of her makeup and shimmied into the flapper dress she'd been working on for two weeks. The silver fabric hugged her minimal curves and fell to the floor in long sheets that made her feel like one of the rich and famous from the 1920s.

She pinned feathers in her hair and stood in front of the full-length mirror in her bedroom to examine her costume. Her mother would most definitely not approve of the thin straps that went over her shoulders, leaving everything else bare. Penny loved the dress though, and she didn't have to check anything off with her mother.

She'd be twenty years old in a couple of months, and if she wanted to wear a spaghetti-strap dress, she could.

She went out into the living room of the apartment and found Hannah and Rob there, sitting close together on the couch, talking. They held hands, and Penny thought they were super cute together.

"Well?" she asked, turning around like a runway model. "What do you think?"

Hannah squealed and jumped up. "I think you look *amazing*, Pen," she said. "I should've had you sew me a dress." She hugged Penny, who giggled with her best friend.

"You're not even dressing up," Penny said, stepping back and adjusting the feathers that had come loose.

"We're going to this church thing," Hannah said, and she sounded less than enthused about it. "We're running the fish pond."

"Oh, for your dad?" Penny asked, looking to Rob. His father ran a congregation in Austin, and Hannah went there for church every week. Penny had been attending with Gideon, and she liked his pastor well enough to keep going. Plus, she liked sitting next to the tall, strong cowboy who held her hand through the sermon. Last week, he'd leaned toward her and asked her to come to his house for lunch afterward.

He'd put a chicken in the slow cooker, and he'd even

managed to peel potatoes and fry them to go with the protein. Penny had been impressed, though she knew Gideon could feed himself. He could go grocery shopping, and pay his bills, and manage his time too. He didn't need her to be his mother, and honestly, that was one of the most refreshing things about him.

"Yeah," Rob said with a sigh as he got up. "We should go, too, Hannah. So we're not late."

"Have fun," Penny said, though Hannah rolled her eyes when Rob turned his back. She smothered the giggle while they left, and then she filled a glass with water and drank, hoping Gideon would show up soon.

He was already late, but Penny had started expecting him to be five to ten minutes late all the time.

When fifteen minutes came, Penny stepped outside. It had cooled considerably in Austin this past week, and she shivered against the night air. It was dark already, and she couldn't help looking toward campus, thinking of the fun they were missing.

She sat on the bottom step near the parking lot, a spot she took up quite often while she waited for him.

She didn't know how much time passed before his headlights cut through the darkness and pulled into a nearby parking spot.

Frustrated, she got up and brushed off her sparkly dress. It didn't hold nearly the same charm as it had inside, and Gideon wouldn't even be able to see her flawless makeup or the details in her hair.

He got out of the truck to greet her, and he wasn't wearing his costume. He grinned all the same, but Penny's stomach plummeted to the tips of her very pointed shoes.

"Look at you, all dressed up." He drew her into a hug, but Penny remained stiff.

"You aren't dressed up."

"I haven't been home yet," he said. "I was thinking I'd get you first since I was so late. Then we could run by my place, where I'd change, and then we'd go."

Penny sighed, because they were already late to the party. Way late. And now they had to go across town to his house and back?

But what could she do about it?

He held the door for her while she climbed into his truck, and they started toward his house.

"You're upset," he said.

"Yes." No sense in denying it. Her annoyance rode on the air like a scent, and Gideon had always been able to name her moods.

"I was waiting for the approval to come through," he said. "They're in California, and it took longer than anyone expected."

"Things always do," she muttered, looking out her window.

"Penny," he said, his voice strong and firm. "We need to talk about this."

"About what?"

"About what sacrifices we're willing to make for one

another." He exhaled. "About supporting each other in our dreams and goals. I need to know what you're willing to do for me, and you need to know what I'm willing to do for you. If it's not good enough, we need to be done."

Shock moved through her. First, no one had ever spoken to her like this. Sure, she'd had other men break up with her; Gideon wouldn't be the first. But their reasons were always things like, "you intimidate me," or "I'm not good enough for you," or "you have way more ambition than I want in a woman."

It had never been because she needed to be more supportive of her boyfriend. They'd always needed to be more accepting and supportive of *her*.

"What do you mean?"

"I mean, I need to know what you're willing to sacrifice to support me in this career I've chosen. You know what I want, just like I know what you want." He made a right turn, and she could detect no anger in him at all. Frustration maybe. "I bring you lunch while you study with another man. I stand up for you to those jerks who have no vision for the future. I've been nothing but proud of you for how hard you work and what you want to do with your life."

"I know that," she said. "You feel like I'm not doing that for you?"

"You're mad at me constantly."

"You're late constantly," she bit back.

"Yes," he said. "I know. Trust me, Penny. I know how

to tell time, and I'm doing the best I can. I haven't cancelled on you in two months. If I'm a little late, that might be your sacrifice."

"What if I don't want that to be my sacrifice?"

"That's exactly what I need to know," he said, stopping at the stop sign. He didn't continue through it. "Tell me right now, Pen. If you can't do that—if you can't accept that I'm going to be late sometimes. Or I might cancel. Or that I really don't even want to go to this stupid party, but I am. I'm willing to go, because *you* want to go—then say it. We'll be done, and I'll get out of your hair. You'll be so much happier."

Penny's heart pounded beneath her breastbone. They got along so well most of the time. He'd told her he was falling for her. They'd looked at diamonds—months ago, but they'd still gone together.

He was willing to end it all, because she got upset when he was half an hour late?

He eased the truck forward, but he didn't continue straight. He started making a wide turn to go back the way they'd come.

"Gideon," she said.

"I think you want me to take you home," he said. "Or to the party? Do you want me to drop you off up there?" He glanced at her, and Penny felt her world dissolving. "Do you have someone you can be with? Get a ride home with? I wouldn't feel right dropping you off alone."

"No," she said softly, but she wasn't sure if she was

telling him she didn't have anyone to spend time with at the party, or if she wanted him to know she didn't want to break up.

Both were true, she supposed.

"Okay, I'll take you home."

"Gideon, I don't want to go home."

"Well, I don't want to go to the party," he said. The rest of the drive happened in silence, and Penny had the distinct feeling she'd be a terrible lawyer if she couldn't even talk to her boyfriend in a straight, forth-coming way.

He pulled up to her building and parked. He didn't get out to open her door like he'd done countless times before. "I'm sorry, sweetheart," he said. "I don't want to do this."

"Then don't," she said.

He just shook his head, and Penny wished he'd say what he was thinking. Perhaps he already had.

"I'll call you, okay?" he asked. When he didn't move or say anything else, Penny had no other choice but to open the door and slide from his truck. "Okay."

She walked away, flinching when his engine roared as he backed out of the space. At the bottom of the steps, she turned and watched his taillights until they turned and she couldn't see them anymore.

15

Gideon put in his time at work. His job, something he'd once loved, felt like drudgery. The technology still excited him, and he'd been put on the lead team to discuss microprocessors and personal computers. He'd been talking to a guy who worked for someone named Steve Jobs, and Gideon had started to wonder if he was with the right company.

Jobs had Big Ideas, and that was the kind of person Gideon wanted to be learning from. The top management at IBM was in another state of flux, and Gideon was glad he was still getting paychecks.

He hated his classes, but he wasn't going to quit now. He hated that he couldn't call Penny and talk to her about it. He'd said he'd call, but he couldn't just pick up where they'd left off, because he'd asked her what she was willing sacrifice, and her answer had been clear.

She either hadn't thought about it or she wasn't willing to put up with him being late. Honestly, he was asking a lot of her, especially with the work she put into things. She'd sewn her entire Halloween costume, and in the few seconds of light he'd seen her in, he knew her makeup had taken time too. A lot of it.

He'd told her he hadn't wanted to go to the party, but he'd been willing to go. Was an hour that big of a deal?

"Obviously," he said as he scrubbed out the kitchen sink. Only a few days had passed, but to Gideon, it felt like years. At the same time, he didn't want to marry Penny only to find out in a year or two years or five that she was so unhappy. He didn't want to deal with a divorce, especially if they had children.

But, oh, how he wanted her children.

He sighed, the job only half done in the kitchen as he laid down his sponge. "This is stupid," he said. "Go talk to her."

His mother's words seemed to be on a loop in his head, and they had been since he'd spoken to her weeks ago. *It takes work. And forgiveness. And a lot of discussion.*

Maybe he'd given up too soon. He'd forced Penny to make an executive decision after two minutes of conversation. That wasn't a lot of discussion.

Gideon washed his hands and checked the clock. Ten-thirty. If Penny stuck to her Saturday schedule, she and Simon had met half an hour ago to study. Gideon knew they had one more test before their final, and that Penny still sat at the top of the chart in the class.

Everyone else knew it now too, and a couple of other boys had asked to join their group. Penny let them all in, and Gideon had tamed his jealousy into a quiet enough beast by taking them lunch and sitting with them for an hour or so before getting on with his life. He'd see Penny on Saturday evenings, and when he kissed her, he never doubted her feelings for him—and only him.

He didn't bother showering. He stopped by Dart's for a dozen doughnuts—not lunch, but it wasn't lunchtime yet —and headed to campus. He'd acted rashly. He needed to have a lot more conversations with Penny before he could simply walk away from her.

He parked and headed toward the square. Penny always chose a table near the library, which overlooked the main square in the center of campus. Gideon had taken one step into the square when he found her group.

Her auburn hair was a siren's call for him, and the way she talked to a man on her right, and then turned to the other one on her left showed her powerful personality. She'd be an excellent mother and a phenomenal lawyer.

They needed to talk about that too. She was still three years from graduating with her Bachelor's degree. Six from law school. They were young, and Gideon would do whatever she wanted, but if they got married soon, they'd have to delay their family for a long time.

Knowing Penny, she'd thought through all of that too, even if they hadn't spoken about it.

Simon caught sight of him first, and he touched Penny's forearm and nodded toward Gideon.

She looked his direction, and Gideon's pulse shot toward the heavens. He should've prayed before he'd left the house. Everything in his life was off-kilter without her in it.

She got up from the table and said something. All three men turned and looked toward Gideon, who slowed his steps and paused a healthy distance away. The last thing he wanted to do was have a serious life discussion with her in front of her study buddies.

She wore a pair of jeans with the perfect flare at the bottom, a pink blouse, and a black jacket over that. She tucked her hands into the jacket as she approached, her eyes flitting around the square like she expected a sneak attack.

"What are you doing here?" she asked, finally looking at him.

Gideon swept his cowboy hat off his head with his free hand. "I brought doughnuts for everyone." He extended the dozen toward her, but she wasn't close enough for him to touch her.

She took the box and stepped back again. "Is that all?"

"No," he said. "I was wondering if you'd be free for dinner tonight."

"With you?"

"Yes," he said, suddenly feeling very inferior. "With me. I'll pick you up nice and proper, and right on time."

Penny met his eyes again, something vulnerable in them. She said nothing.

"I miss you, Penny," he said. "I'm sorry I made it a make-or-break moment the other day. We need more discussion. I do think we need to talk about all of this, though, and I want to."

She nodded. "I miss you too."

"I'm in love with you," he blurted out. "I hope we can come to a place where we'll both be happy. Not just me, and not just you, but both of us."

Penny reached up and swiped at her eyes. "You're in love with me?"

"Helplessly," he said, half miserable and half hopeful.

She sobbed and lunged toward him. He caught her around the waist and held her as tightly as he could. "I'm sorry," he said. "I'm so sorry. Please forgive me."

"I don't want you to think I'm mad at you all the time," she said, her voice pitchy. "You don't deserve that, and I don't want to be your mother."

"I hate disappointing you," he said. "I do, Pen. It's the worst thing in the world for me. I'm trying to figure out how to be the man you deserve—one with a job and a good wage and helpful too—and the Gideon who wants to invent something the entire world will use."

"Let me go talk to my group," she said. "And we'll go right now." She backed up a step.

"Really? You don't need to study?"

She looked at him, her bright green eyes intense and passionate. "You're more important. I'll be right back."

Gideon watched her go, feeling gratitude and relief mix together inside him. He wasn't sure he deserved a woman like Penny, but he'd been steadily falling for her since the moment his eyes had met hers. He'd never been so grateful his dogs were disobedient, and that Penny had been in that park, at that moment.

Gideon's faith in a loving God renewed as Penny packed up her books and said goodbye to her friends. When she faced him again, he saw the adoration on her face.

She ran the last few steps to him, and she dropped her backpack at his feet. "I should've said this a few minutes ago, but I was afraid."

Gideon ran his fingers down the side of her face. "We can't be afraid to say things to each other. We get to. Anything we're struggling with. Anything that's bothering us."

Penny nodded along to everything he said. "I love you, Gideon. These last few days have been horrible for me. Watching you drive away from me—I never want to go through that again."

Gideon's heart expanded and expanded and expanded. "So we love each other."

"Seems like it." A giant grin spread across her face. "Now what?"

"I went and saw my mother a couple of weeks ago," he said, taking her hand. He turned so he was walking the same way as her, and they started to stroll across the square. "She said we have to talk a lot. Discuss what we're willing to sacrifice to support each other. That's why I asked you that the other night." He hung his head, foolishness racing through him. "I didn't mean to push you into a place where we weren't talking at all. I was just frustrated. I do *not* want to fail you, sweetheart. Ever."

"Gideon, that's unreasonable," she said gently. "You're going to fail. I'm going to fail. The important thing is what we do when that happens."

"Can't drive away," he muttered. "I should've called."

"I could've called you too," she said. "I know your number."

He looked at her, and he saw all the way into her soul. She was kind, and good, and exactly the right woman for him. "So I won't drive away again. We'll keep talking, and we'll keep looking toward a future together. When we're ready, I'll buy you the best ring I can afford, and we'll get married."

Her smile could've lit the entire country. "And then we'll have those kids." She paused and reached up to touch him, right above where his heart thumped in his chest. "I want to have your children, Gideon."

"As many as the Good Lord will give us," he said, smiling at her too. He bent down, wishing they'd found a bit more privacy on this campus. He paused, his lips about to touch hers. "I sure am in love with you, Penny Aarons."

"I sure am in love with you too, Gideon Walker."

They laughed together, and then Gideon did kiss her, not caring one whit who saw them.

———

Read on for a sneak peek at the first of Penny and Gideon's sons - **RHETT.**

I've also included the first *two chapters* of FOUR of my other bestselling books so you can sample them and choose the story you're most interested in reading.

Sneak Peek! Rhett - Chapter One

"It's totally fine," Evelyn Foster said to the woman on the other end of the line. "Not every first date goes well." She often had to counsel her clients through a few dates before they could see what she saw.

Being a small-town matchmaker, where ninety percent of the men were cowboys, wasn't an easy job. But Evelyn loved it, as she could make everything line up on paper like a dream. The women knew what she was doing, but the men...well, sometimes men just needed to get out of their own way.

And Evelyn provided a way for them to do that—and conveniently run into the woman of their dreams. They just didn't know it yet.

And obviously, Tina didn't know it yet either. "He's perfect for you," Evelyn assured her. "What happened that rubbed you the wrong way?"

"For starters, he wanted to take me to the big box store for a date."

Evelyn could hear the eyeroll in Tina's voice.

"But you persuaded him to do something else, right?" Evelyn asked, shuffling a couple of pages on the desk in front of her. The wind shook the windows of her office, and she glanced outside to see a dust storm had kicked up on the farm where she lived with her sisters.

Granted, they didn't really use the two hundred acres they had, as that was a lot for three women to manage by themselves. Their father had retired a few years ago, and they mostly planted as much as they could and sold the hay to other farms and ranches surrounding Three Rivers.

"I did, yes," Tina said. "But is that going to be my whole life moving forward? Me trying to persuade this guy to do what I want?"

"Let me look through a few more candidates," Evelyn said, focusing on her papers again. May was an exceptionally busy time for her services, as well as around the Shining Star Ranch. While her oldest sister, Callie, ran most of what happened on the ranch, Evelyn had plenty of chores to do too. "And I'll get back to you in a couple of days, okay?"

"Okay," Tina said. "What should I do if Gideon calls?"

"You get to decide that," Evelyn said, looking at Gideon's one-sheet. "He really does seem perfect for you.

Maybe he just didn't want to commit to something as long as dinner."

"I don't know how that's a plus," Tina said dryly.

"Well, he's met you once, for what? Five minutes at the dry cleaner? Somewhere I only knew he'd be because we got a last-minute phone call." Evelyn never revealed her sources, but she had spies all over the town of Three Rivers.

With a population of almost seventeen thousand now, she certainly couldn't be everywhere at once, or know where every eligible bachelor would be at any given time.

"And that was the first time he'd been there," Evelyn reminded her. "So maybe give him a little slack?" She spoke as kindly as she could. After all, Tina was paying her, and she didn't need to lose a client because the cowboy Tina had her eye on was out of his element.

"Okay." Tina sighed. "But still look at a couple of other guys for me."

"Anyone in mind?" Evelyn asked, because no one else on her list stood out for someone like Tina. She liked a through-and-through Texas cowboy, with a big hat, and the biggest belt buckle possible. Rodeo experience a plus.

While there were plenty of cowboys in Three Rivers, Tina wanted Cowboy Extreme.

"I've seen a man at church the last few weeks," Tina said. "He looks new in town."

Evelyn repressed a sigh and looked out the window again. She couldn't see the trees she knew were only ten feet away. Alarms started sounding in her mind, and surprise darted through her that she hadn't lost cell phone reception yet.

"I don't know his name or where he lives," Tina said.

"All right," Evelyn said. "I'll put out some feelers to find out who this guy is." With that, the line crackled, and Tina's words broke up. In the next moment, the service cut out, and Evelyn looked at her phone to see the call had indeed been severed.

"Great," she muttered. Now she had to hunt down a mystery cowboy who was new to town. Maybe Patrick would know. Her boyfriend worked the meat counter at the grocery store, and he saw a lot of people—especially single cowboys coming to buy their steak dinners.

Of course, a lot of the cowboys around Three Rivers worked on farms and ranches, and they often got plenty of beef for free from their employers. So maybe Patrick wouldn't know. But it couldn't hurt to ask him.

He knew what Evelyn did for a living, and he often sent her texts with information on men she needed to know about. She couldn't send him a text right then, as it seemed her provider had gone down with the crazy windstorm.

She left her office at the same time a horrible, glass-shattering sound filled the whole farmhouse. She screamed, hers matching her younger sister's in the living room.

Callie burst in the back door with the words, "There's

a tornado headed this way. Come help me with the animals." She spun away before either Evelyn or Simone could answer.

Thankfully, Evelyn already had shoes on, and she hurried after her oldest sister, saying, "The sirens haven't even gone off. Maybe it's just a windstorm."

The moment she finished speaking, the chilling, distinct wail of the tornado siren filled the air.

She ran after Callie, who handed her a grease pen and a handful of fly masks. "Put our phone number on their sides. Put on the fly mask, and we'll set them in the pasture."

They didn't have the hurricane clips or reinforced beams needed to tether the horses securely in the barn, and their horses were used to roaming in pastures.

"Maybe it'll go north," Callie said, her voice panicked. "Like that last one."

The last tornado had been over two years ago, and it had indeed turned north before inflicting too much damage on Three Rivers. She handed Simone the same items she had Evelyn, and the sisters got to work.

"We have to go next door, too," Callie said. "We'll put our number on the animals at Fox Hill for the new owner."

"Who is it?" Evelyn asked, glancing east though she couldn't see more than five feet in either direction. Even Callie's voice coming through the swirling dirt and dust felt eerie and otherworldly.

"Some guy," Callie said vaguely, which meant she

didn't know either. "Last name's Walker, I think. Mason texted a couple of days ago and said he'd be here this week, and that we could turn the keys over to him then."

Mason Martin had lived and cultivated Fox Hill Ranch next door for years and years before deciding to up and move to Hawaii, of all places. He'd put the ranch up for sale, and contracted with the sisters to take care of the few animals he'd left behind. He had a staff of four still on the premises too, and Evelyn wondered why they couldn't take care of their own horses.

"What about Orion?" she asked. "Can't he turn the horses out to pasture over there?" It was at least a half-mile to Fox Hill, though their properties touched one another along a fence line on the east side of the ranch. Evelyn did *not* want to get caught out in the storm.

"They went into town this morning," Callie said, finishing with her last horse, smacking it on the flank and saying, "Go on. Stay safe."

With their own livestock numbered and protected as much as possible, the three sisters piled into Callie's pickup truck and rumbled down the road. If anything, the wind blew stronger at Fox Hill, but Evelyn kept her head down and her fingers moving as she marked the eight horses Mason had left behind.

He also had two pigs, six goats, and a whole herd of chickens. The tornado would likely pick them up and carry them off, and she certainly didn't know how to hold one long enough to write a phone number on feathers.

With all the animals marked that could be, Callie shouted, "We have to go inside!"

Exactly what Evelyn didn't want to do, at least not here. But one look at the sky, and she knew she didn't have a choice. Panic filled her, though she'd lived through tornadoes before. They weren't super common in this area of Texas, but she'd had enough experience with them to know what to do in case of an emergency.

"Where's Daddy?" Simone asked.

"He's with Granny," Callie yelled, holding her hat on her head as she ran for the back door of Mason's homestead.

It felt strangely quiet inside, with the three of them panting as they sucked at air that finally wasn't filled with debris.

"Come on," Callie said. "He'll have a tornado shelter."

Evelyn had been to Mason's house several times, and she knew right where it was. As Callie turned to go down a hallway, she said, "It's over here, guys. He showed it to me once." She hated that she wasn't in her own home, protecting it and herself.

But just inside the living room off the front door, she swept aside the rug and pointed to the hatch door there. "Goes down into a cement foundation."

"Get in," Callie said as glass broke somewhere in the house. The tornado might not strike Three Rivers directly, but this wind was definitely wicked and causing some real damage.

Evelyn went first and turned on her phone's flashlight. Callie followed and did the same, with Simone bringing up the rear. No sooner had Simone closed the door above them and come down the steps did it open again.

Callie shone her flashlight on the man sliding down the steps, pure fear in every line on his face. "Who are you?" she asked as Evelyn swung her light onto him too.

He bore a strong jaw and dark eyes—exactly the kind of man Evelyn would be interested in. You know, if she wasn't already dating someone.

The stranger drew in a deep breath and spoke in an even deeper voice. "I'm Rhett Walker. This is my ranch." He dusted himself off with a pair of big hands and added, "You must be the Foster sisters from next door."

"Guilty," Callie said, lowering her light so it wasn't shining right in Rhett's face. But Evelyn couldn't do the same. His good looks and bass voice seemed to have frozen her to the spot, and all she could do was stare while her heart pounded wildly in her chest.

"Can you stop shining that in my face?" he asked, his voice a touch colder than before, and Callie put her hand on Evelyn's arm to make her put the phone down.

"So," he said with only the soft glow on his features now. He was somehow sexier and more beautiful than in the harsh light, and Evelyn wondered where in the world all these thoughts and feelings were coming from. "I guess the tornado is welcoming me to the Texas Panhandle." He laughed, and Simone and Callie joined him.

Evelyn simply reveled in the sound of his laughter, thinking that if she weren't with Patrick, she'd definitely be setting herself up with one cowboy Rhett Walker.

Callie started to detail what they'd done for his animals and why they'd come in his house instead of theirs, and Evelyn shied behind her sister so she could continue to simply stare at her new next-door neighbor.

Sneak Peek! Rhett - Chapter Two

Rhett Walker could not believe his rotten luck. It seemed like he'd run into a string of it, and he wondered when it would end. Just like this blasted tornado. It seemed to go on for a long time, and not only because he was trapped in his own storm shelter with three strangers.

Women, sure, but they chatted more with each other than him. He'd switched on the flashlight on his phone and currently stood in front of a long shelf with dozens of cans on it. At least they wouldn't starve down here.

"How do you know when the tornado is over?" he asked, thinking he needed a camera that showed the weather outside so he wouldn't have to risk losing his hat to check. He felt six eyes on him, but when he turned, only one woman still stared at him.

"Evelyn, right?" he asked, taking a step closer to her.

"Right," she said, her voice hoarse. She coughed, and Rhett watched her. "Sorry," she added. "We were out in the dust and dirt for a while before coming in." She cleared her throat and bent down to a lower shelf.

She straightened and held two bottles of water in her hand. "Do you mind if I have one of these?" She extended the second one toward him, and he took it.

"No problem."

"Where are you from? Have you been in a lot of tornadoes?"

"I grew up outside of Austin?" Why he phrased it like a question, he wasn't sure. He found himself clearing his own throat, as if this woman made him nervous. Everything about coming out to a ranch made him squirm a little, and three of his brothers were supposed to be with him. But there had been some problems at the office a couple of days ago, and he'd ended up coming north himself.

"I know where Austin is," Evelyn said with a small smile. She hid it behind the water bottle as she drank.

Of course she did, and suddenly the storm shelter felt a little too hot. He returned his attention to the shelves in front of him. "My father owned a technology company there," he said, glancing at her. "This shelter needs one of his cameras, then we'd know when the tornado has passed."

"You'll be able to tell," she said. "Even without a camera."

"You think so?" He wasn't sure how, as it wasn't like there were any windows in the shelter.

"A camera would get knocked around in a storm," she said, cocking her head at him, the questions clear.

Rhett shuffled his feet, but he kept his eyes on hers. "My dad had contracts with the military and government," he said. "The cameras were tiny."

"Tiny? How tiny?"

"Pinhead tiny," he said. "The wind wouldn't knock it off." As if the world had been holding its breath and had just released it, something changed. He looked up to the ceiling, the lack of groaning evident. "I think the storm is over."

"It's passing," one of Evelyn's sisters said, and Rhett couldn't believe that she could tell without visual proof. "Let's give it a few more minutes," the other woman said.

"Callie," Evelyn said, providing Rhett with the name he'd forgotten, though they'd only been in the shelter for maybe ten minutes. "She's the oldest," she added in a mock whisper, and Rhett got the message.

A chuckle started in the back of his throat, and he ducked his head as he tried to quiet it. "A little bossy, is that what you're saying?"

"She has moments," Evelyn said, and Rhett met her eyes again. She had a beautiful smile to go with that long, dark hair and those sparkling eyes. He couldn't really tell what color those were in the glow of flashlights, and he told his heart to stop skipping beats.

He hadn't bought this ranch out in the middle of nowhere to get his heart broken again. He'd managed to do that in Austin, thank you very much.

"I'm the oldest," Rhett said. "Six younger brothers."

"Wow," Evelyn said, those eyes still shining at him. "I thought some of them were coming with you."

"They are," he said. "The twins got held up in Austin, tying up loose ends, but I had to come up for the job."

She cocked her head again. "The ranch is fine."

"Oh, Jeremiah is going to mostly be doing the ranch stuff," he said. "I'll help a little. The twins are technology dudes, but they insisted on coming." He shrugged, because Tripp and Liam didn't even own plaid shirts.

"So what's the job?" she asked.

"I'm a forensic veterinarian," he said. "There's a case up here that's expected to take a while. My dad's company was selling, and this place was for sale...." He let the words hang there.

Evelyn's eyes narrowed. "Have you ever lived on a ranch?"

Before he had to answer that, Callie said, "I'm going up." That caused movement, and while Evelyn watched him for an extra moment, she too moved toward the ladder. He let them all go up first, feeling like perhaps he should've done so to make sure no one got hurt.

Thankfully, the house still stood at the top of the ladder, though there were several windows broken.

"Looks bad," Callie said, walking over the dirt that had been blown in through the broken windows.

"This is bad?" Rhett asked, not quite the house and ranch tour he'd been expecting. The weight of the clean-up felt like tons and tons, and he couldn't shoulder it. He stood in the middle of the kitchen, turning slowly.

The appliances were still there. Countertops. Even the kitchen table and barstools.

The women had gone out the back door, and Rhett went out onto the deck as well. He had so many questions, and he'd been hoping he could ask the four men who supposedly lived here on this ranch he'd bought.

Only Evelyn paused at the edge of the lawn and lifted her hand in a friendly wave, and Rhett returned it. Then she turned and followed her sisters, their red pickup firing up and rumbling down the road to the west, where their ranch obviously was.

He sighed and looked up into the still angry sky. "Really, Lord? A tornado? What am I supposed to do now?"

He had the very strong feeling that he better get to work, so he went into the garage and found a broom. After all, God had led him here, and he couldn't leave now.

RHETT HAD MOST of the main floor swept out when his phone rang. "Hello?" He didn't recognize the number, but he had a feeling he'd be answering a lot of calls from people he didn't know in the near future.

"Mister Walker?" a cowboy drawled.

"Yep, you got 'im," he said.

"I'm Orion Goldberg," the other cowboy said. "We got stuck in town and wondered where you ended up during the tornado. Maybe you're not in town yet?"

"I'm at Fox Hill," he said, pushing the huge pile of dirt out onto the deck. Everywhere he looked, there was more work to do, as evidenced by the patio table and chairs his eyes caught on. The umbrella was still there, but bent, and a sigh passed through his whole soul.

"Arrived just before the tornado. Good news," he said, trying to find the silver lining in this situation, the way his mother had always done. "The storm shelter is stocked with food and fits four people." With room for more.

"Four people?"

"The women from down the road were here," Rhett said, thinking immediately of Evelyn. He consciously switched his thoughts to how he needed to rename the ranch now that he'd finally arrived.

Just another thing in a long to-do list.

"Well, we're still in Three Rivers," Orion said, his voice fading for a moment. "What do you need us to bring back? How'd the windows fare? The animals?"

Jeremiah was supposed to be here to run the ranch, and Rhett had paid little attention to the type and number of animals on the ranch.

"Uh...." He looked out over the land behind the homestead and found several outbuildings. Barns and stables and coops. He turned away from them, overwhelmed and thankful for the four men who would be back soon. Hopefully. "There are several broken windows. Dirt and stuff everywhere. I'm sweeping out the house now."

"We'll bring back lumber and some cleaning supplies. What about groceries?"

"Can I call something in?" Rhett asked, turning back to the house. He'd bought the ranch a couple of months ago, but he and his brothers hadn't made the move immediately. The owner had said his neighbors and the crew at Fox Hill could manage for a while, and they obviously had.

"To where?" Orion asked, and that answered Rhett's question. It only took fifteen minutes to drive into the town of Three Rivers, and it was a bustling place. At least Mason Martin had told him it was. Rhett had come straight to the ranch when he'd seen the windstorm kick up and the sky turn an ugly shade of green.

"Never mind," he said.

"We can bring out some food, boss," Orion said, and Rhett wasn't used to being the boss. He worked for the state as a forensic veterinarian, and while there were only a few people who did what he did, he wasn't the boss.

"That would be great," he said. If they wanted him to be the boss, he could do it. "I'll pay you back." He outlined a few grocery staples for Orion, and the call ended. As he swept the dirt back onto the ground where it belonged, he supposed things at Fox Hill could be worse. He could be the only one here, with no money to pay for anything.

As it was, he had a crew coming back with the supplies he needed, and his brothers on their way. Oh, and plenty of money, as when his father had sold the company he'd built, he'd gotten billions for it.

All the Walker brothers now had billions too—which was how Rhett had gotten this ranch in the first place. It was the second-biggest one in the area, and well-maintained. At least it had been.

"And it will be again," Rhett vowed. "But it needs a new name. A fresh start." Just like him and his brothers.

"So what do we call it?" he mused aloud to himself, not quite used to so much country stillness and silence. He and three of his brothers would be living here. "Four...." The only word he could think of was men, and that sounded stupid.

Plus, once Wyatt finished with the rodeo circuit, he'd probably come to the ranch too. With Rhett's parents retired and living in Grand Cayman now, there was no "home" for the rodeo king to return to.

"Seven Sons," Rhett said, the name popping into his head. It fit. It was perfect, and while Rhett certainly hadn't appreciated all of the rotten luck that had brought him to this part of Texas, he tipped his head back and looked up into the clearing sky.

"Thank you, Lord," he whispered, because he at least

had a place to stay, money to fund the rebuilding of this place, and family coming.

He didn't need a wife, despite what his mother said. Oh, no, he did not.

———

Could their make-believe marriage be exactly what they both need to get out of their own way and find a happily-ever-after?

Read RHETT today to find out! Scan the QR code to grab him.

Keep reading for a sneak peek of **SECOND CHANCE RANCH**.

Sneak Peek! Second Chance Ranch Chapter One

The walls in Kelly Russell's life had never seemed so close. Of course, they hadn't been this putrid shade of yellow for a long time, either. Her parents lived with the motto of "use it up, wear it out, make it do, or do without," and kitchen wall paint was no exception.

But if Kelly could ace this morning's job interview, she had a chance of getting her own walls again. Soon. And she'd paint them. Maybe blue, or purple, or green. Something cool. Anything but the stark white she'd had in California—or this dark yellow.

"I have to drive out to the ranch." She straightened her jacket as she glanced toward her mom and son, who sat at the kitchen table eating breakfast. She'd sailed through her college admissions interview in this jacket. She'd been hired for her first real job in this jacket. She'd also worn this jacket in divorce court and been granted full custody of her son, Finn.

She hoped the turquoise number would work its magic today. She tugged down the hemline, wondering when her black skirt had gotten a smidge too small.

Probably while you were sitting on the beach these past five years. She knew there'd be no sitting at Three Rivers Ranch, though she hoped the accountant would at least have an office.

"It's about twenty-five miles on that old, dirt road," she continued, knowing her four-year-old son wasn't listening, but hoping her mother was. "So I'll be gone for, I don't know, at least two hours. Maybe three."

"We'll be fine," her mom said. "I've taken care of children before."

"I know." Kelly pressed her lips together and determined that she did not need another layer of lipstick. She'd slick on clear gloss just before the interview. "But it's been a long time."

It had been twenty-four years, to be exact, since Kelly had been four. And her mother didn't seem as sharp as she once had.

Her dad grumped his way into the kitchen, but Kelly knew his frowny face was an act. "Hey, Finny," he said. "Want to go throw the pigskin?"

"Just a second, Daddy." Kelly crouched down and drew her son into a hug. "Love you, baby. Be good for Grandma and Grandpa."

She stood, and a sliver of nervous energy ran through her as she thought about returning to the ranch she'd loved as a teenager. She could practically smell the dust, hear the horses whinnying, and picture her best friend waving from the front porch, though Chelsea lived in Dallas now.

"Three Rivers needs a new financial controller," her mom said as she walked with Kelly to the front door. "You're qualified, and Frank knows you. He'd have to be dead not to hire you."

"Didn't you say he was going to be retiring soon?" Kelly worried the inside of her bottom lip with her teeth.

"That's what Glenda said." Mom put both hands on Kelly's shoulders as Kelly pictured the ladies down at the hair salon gossiping about everything from the price of beef to who'd moved in over the weekend. "You've got this." Her mom nodded and released her.

A rush of appreciation lifted Kelly's lips into a smile. "Thanks, Mom."

As she drove away from her childhood home, she made a mental list of things she could thank her parents for. Giving her a fabulous childhood under the wide, Texas sky. Paying for fifteen years of dance classes, which had provided her with a skill she'd used to fund her college education. Teaching her how to laugh.

Allowing her and Finn to take over their basement after her divorce.

She thought of her work at the local grocer as she pointed her pathetic excuse for a car toward the ranch.

She'd been back in Three Rivers for several weeks, and she'd taken the first job she could get. But ringing up milk didn't pay well enough for her to buy her own house and raise a child. And the nearest dance studio was in Amarillo, fifty miles away. The investment of time and money to get there and back didn't make teaching ballet a viable option.

Kelly's fingers tightened on the steering wheel. "I've got this," she repeated. The gently rolling hills calmed her, as they always had. She'd spent countless hours out here with nothing but her thoughts, the wind, and her friends. The open, blue sky further anchored her. She'd loved lying on her back in Chelsea's backyard, creating stories from the clouds that rolled by. And the summer storms—she and Chelsea had made up their own songs, their own lyrics, their own choreography, all to the sound of thunder.

By the time she turned down the dirt driveway that led to the homestead, a sense of peace filled her. This ranch had been her second home growing up, and coming back to it now felt right. If she could get this job, it would be the first step toward getting her whole life back.

The nerves returned. She took a deep breath at the sight of the familiar house, imposing the first time you saw it. But Kelly knew better. She'd been in every room, felt the love and warmth from the family pictures hanging on the walls.

Kelly laughed at the memory at the same time her chest squeezed. Working at Three Rivers would provide a little safety at a time when Kelly had none. No pressure or anything.

She noted the American flag flying in the front yard of the ranch-style home. She'd kept in touch with Chelsea over the years and knew her younger brother, Squire, had joined the Army. His mother was obviously proud.

Kelly wondered if she'd get to see Heidi today, maybe experience one of her powder-scented hugs. A nostalgic smile played at her lips. She hoped so.

She left the house behind as she drove to the edge of the homestead, passing the barns, stables, and grain towers. Three industrial trailers edged the property before it gave way to the bull yards, and Kelly parked next to a row of dirty trucks, her little sedan a miniature vehicle among the bulky ranch equipment.

She glanced around as she walked through the packed-dirt parking lot, noticing that not much had changed. The clucking of chickens and the lowing of cattle met her ears, attributes that indicated this was indeed a working ranch. Kelly sidestepped a particularly large stone in the path. She'd have dust all the way to her knees by the time she made it inside. Everything about her spoke of a city businesswoman entering a whole new world, but she'd had to wear her heels. This was an *interview*.

Unfortunately, the metal steps and ramp were grated, creating a veritable gauntlet for her Jimmy Choo's. She supposed the heels, though fashionable and absolutely the perfect statement for this outfit, weren't exactly ranch attire.

She shifted her weight onto the balls of her feet and made it up four steps before her right heel sank through the metal. She set down her purse and tried to wrench the shoe free as she balanced on her toes. The Texas heat caused a trickle of sweat to form on her forehead. She did not want to enter the interview dusty, heelless, and now sticky.

She swung her hair over her shoulder, the movement throwing her off-balance. She gripped the railing to steady herself and prepared to make another attempt at freeing her shoe.

"You know, most ranch hands wear boots," a man said behind her.

Kelly's heart tripped as a strangled sound came out of her throat. She straightened, her hand smoothing down the back of her skirt, where a high slit was located. Had he seen anything?

She pressed her eyes closed. She'd never felt out of place on this ranch, and she wasn't going to start now. "Yes, I can see why," she agreed. "However, I didn't get the memo." Kelly opened her eyes and twisted to see who she'd need to avoid on the ranch. Because she was going to get this job, sweaty, mismatched, and dirty notwithstanding. She expected to see a cowboy—preferably one with a multi-purpose tool he could use to cut her free.

But this man, standing over six feet tall, didn't wear the regular stonewashed jeans and long-sleeved shirt. No siree. Not a boot or a belt buckle was in sight. Instead his pressed khakis and black polo accentuated his athletic body. Biceps strained against the sleeves of his shirt, a clear testament that ranching did a body good. Maybe he drank a gallon of milk everyday too. The only two indicators that he belonged in Texas were the cowboy hat perched naturally on his head and the panting dog at his side.

Kelly's reasons for wanting the position suddenly shifted to a completely new level. She gave herself a mental shake—she needed a job, not a boyfriend.

"Ma'am." He took off his hat and ran his fingers through his thick, brown hair. She couldn't tell from his sly smile and the amused sparkle in his eye if he was secretly laughing at her predicament or if he'd seen way more leg than she'd intended. She found herself returning his devilish smirk. Why was her stomach doing that floaty thing? She suppressed it and smoothed her hand over the back of her skirt again.

As he settled his hat back on his head, Kelly twisted and slid her feet out of the toes of her shoes. She turned around carefully so as to avoid touching the jagged metal, and placed her feet back on her shoes. Good thing she'd taken all those dance lessons. Still, her calf muscles hadn't been used this way for a long time.

As she took in his form again, she recognized his cobalt

blue eyes still sparking with mischief, his straight, long nose, and his square jaw where that smile remained.

"Squire?" She wobbled a little as she spoke.

He seemed startled at the use of his name, his smile fading. Squire studied her for a moment, thunderclouds darkening his eyes into a shade of gray that reminded Kelly of the churning ocean. "I don't think we've met," he said.

Oh, they had. He just possessed a lot more to admire now than he had in high school, including a pair of unforgettable dimples that appeared as his grin returned. "Are you going to clue me in?" he asked. "Or just stare at me until your name appears in my mind?" He folded his arms across his broad chest and quirked his eyebrows.

She blinked rapidly, embarrassed that she'd been caught gawking. "I'm Kelly Russell." She shook her head, wishing she could shake away the words just as easily. "I mean Armstrong. Kelly Armstrong."

"Like, Bond. James Bond?" His throaty laugh tickled her ears. "Sorry. Doesn't ring a bell."

He shrugged like it was no big deal that he didn't remember her. Kelly couldn't understand how he could've forgotten. She'd practically lived down the hall in his sister's room.

"Yeah," she said, still balancing backward in her shoes, the heel still jammed into the metal steps. "Remember, I was on the cheer squad with Chelsea? I slept over here all the time?" She peered at him, but his face remained impassive, stoic.

"Chelsea had a lot of friends," he said. "Were you one of the gigglers?"

"No!" Kelly blew her hair out of her eyes, but it stuck to her forehead. She gave up hope of going into the interview without a bucket of sweat dripping from her face. "Remember how we used to choreograph dances and make you judge us?" Kelly emitted a nervous giggle before she could quell the sound.

"You just wanted to watch football, and we'd drag you into the backyard and make you watch us do our high kicks." She attempted the move now, realizing too late that her skirt was too tight for such things. Her foot barely made it above her knee and that slit allowed a blast of air to go up her skirt.

Squire's eyes closed briefly as she pressed down her clothes once more. The dog whined, somehow sensing her stupidity and warning her to *stop now!*

She'd lost her mind. *So this is what it feels like*, she thought. She'd let Squire completely undo her composure. Still, it bothered her that he didn't remember her. She took a deep breath, trying to refocus on the impending interview.

"Okay, well, whatever. Maybe you can help me get out of this mess." She pointed at her shoe and tried for a carefree chuckle. It sounded more like a strangled cat. At least it wasn't a giggle.

Squire joined her on the fourth step, steadying her as she turned around and stepped back into her shoes properly. "Why don't you just take off the shoe and then yank it out?" He released her and continued up the stairs while his dog slipped past them to lie in the shade. "In fact, I would've removed my shoes first, climbed the steps and then put them back on. At least shoes like that." He gave her a flirtatious wink, and her memory stumbled. Maybe this man wasn't Squire Ackerman. Kelly had certainly never seen him with more muscles in his body than stars in the sky. And he'd never flirted with her.

"I'd like to see you wear shoes like this," she muttered, her gaze murderous as she glared at him.

"I would *rock* shoes like that, darlin'," he said. "And Kelly? I remember your high kick being much...higher."

Her heart cartwheeled through her chest. He did know who she was! That little snake.

Before she could formulate an answer, he entered the building and let the door crash closed behind him.

"Take the shoe off, *darlin'*," she mimicked, but she did what Squire had suggested. The metal was just as hot and ragged as it looked. She balanced on the ball of her foot, trying to do as little damage as possible, this time to her skin. Her heel came free, and thankfully, it had only suffered a few minor scrapes.

"Is he always like that?" she asked his border collie, but he simply looked at her with a pleading expression, as if to say, *Please don't attempt that high kick again.* She vaguely recognized the animal, but she couldn't recall his name. She did remember that Squire had always loved his dogs. "Bet he'd help you if you got stuck."

She removed her other shoe and scampered up the rest of the steps barefoot. As she slipped back into her heels on the safety of the rubber mat outside the door, Kelly wiped her brow, sent a prayer heavenward that she could ace this interview, and took a deep breath. Then she pushed open the door.

———

Squire Ackerman winced at the sound of the door banging closed behind him, the metal on metal reminding him of being trapped in the tank. Immediately, the smell of hot gears and diesel fuel assaulted him, though the more accurate scent in the administration trailer would be men who worked with horses.

He took a moment to center himself, grateful he'd managed to navigate the stairs and enter the building without Kelly seeing his limp. As he strode down the aisle toward the ranch hands, he wasn't as successful. He'd been back at Three Rivers long enough for them to get used to his somewhat stunted gait, and they all busied themselves as they sensed his approaching fury.

"Where's Ethan?" he growled at Tom Lovell, the only cowboy who hadn't found a pretended task upon Squire's arrival.

"Sent him out to the north fence, Boss." Tom's gum snapped as he chewed it. "You said it had popped its rungs."

"How long's he been gone?"

"He left about seven." Tom stared steadily back at Squire, something the Army major appreciated. *Tom would make a good general controller*, Squire thought. But Clark sat at the front desk, and he'd run the operations on the ranch for almost as long as Squire had been alive.

Squire grunted his acceptance of Tom's answer and hurried around the short, semi-permanent partition. The shoulder-height wall separated the front area of the trailer, where the cowboys met and received their assignments, from the row of permanent offices he'd built into the back.

His father's door was the first on the left, Squire's second, and their accountant occupied the last office.

He might as well start thinking of it as Kelly's. Squire knew his father had already hired her in his mind. The interview was simply a formality.

Squire's phone buzzed in his front pocket, but he waited until he'd made it inside his office, shut the door, and flipped the lock. Only then did he remove his phone, already knowing who had texted. Squire sighed, wishing he'd never taught his mother how to use technology.

Has Kelly arrived?

Like she didn't have her nose pressed against the front windows, watching and waiting for Kelly's car, simply so she could text him about it. She'd also sent message after message last night, each asking if Squire could handle seeing Kelly again. Her last one had said, *Forget about last time. This is your second chance.*

He'd ignored all her messages until that one. Then he'd sent back, *There was no last time, and there is no this time. Mom, stop!*

He definitely wanted there to be a *last* time. His invitation to her senior prom proved that. Her rejection screamed through him as loudly now as it had a decade ago. There would definitely *not* be a *this time.*

He leaned against the locked door and closed his eyes.

She hadn't driven the forty minutes to the ranch to find a new husband, he knew that for certain. He couldn't let the lines between them blur like they had last time.

At least he'd assigned Ethan a task in a remote quarter of the ranch. A calculated move, since Squire knew Ethan was the best looking cowboy employed at the ranch, with the biggest ego. He would've hit on Kelly before she even made it into his father's office. Squire had sent him away to protect her from Ethan—not because he was jealous or worried about the competition. Definitely not because of that.

Squire knew the moment Kelly entered the building, and not only from the way the walls vibrated as the door slammed shut. That sound would never become familiar, and Squire blinked away the blinding images of smoke rising from a mangled heap of metal that used to be a tank. The one driven by Lou.

Though dangerous, he focused on what he could remember about Kelly to help drive away the memories of his last deployment. The scent of her perfume had stuck with him through the years. As he'd passed her on the stairs, he'd caught the same whiff of cocoa butter and honeysuckle he'd always associated with her.

Kelly's voice floated through the thin walls of his office. "Thank you, Tom." Squire stuffed away the twinge of guilt that he'd caused her embarrassment. *He* hadn't worn impractical footwear to the ranch.

The walls shook again, Squire's signal that his dad had arrived. He'd expect Squire in the interview, though he'd already decided to hire Kelly. Squire didn't understand the point of the interview if he was going to hire the first person who walked through the door.

She's the only *person*, he reminded himself. Still, she'd barely made it *through* the door, what with those ridiculous shoes. He'd had to employ his military training to keep his face blank while he'd spoken to her.

Pretending he didn't know her may have been childish. Crossing his arms made him appear imposing and big, and he knew it. He'd done both on purpose to keep her at arm's length. He hated that she turned him to mush with a tropical scent and a smattering of freckles.

He took a cleansing breath, praying for the strength he lacked. He'd experienced plenty of frustrating situations during his dual deployments overseas. He could weather this too, especially since Kelly Armstrong had made her interest clear years ago. Nothing between them had changed. He was still Chelsea's little brother, someone Kelly had overlooked so often Squire had felt so completely invisible he'd sometimes startled when she spoke to him.

His phone buzzed again, but he chucked it on his desk before yanking open the door and heading toward his father's office, taking careful seconds to make sure his left leg didn't outpace his right.

Squire studied Kelly from a distance before he entered the room. Her turquoise blazer gave her a feminine figure, with a white blouse barely visible underneath. She wore those four-inch black heels and just the right amount of makeup to be professional. Her sandy hair fell halfway down her back; her light green eyes were as magnetic now as they'd been ten years ago.

He crossed his arms. A stampede of raging bulls did not scare Squire Ackerman. Bad weather could not deter him. Women did not affect him.

Major Squire Ackerman had complete control over himself, his emotions, and what he let other people see.

Especially Kelly.

"I am fearless," he heard her say as he stepped closer to the doorway. "Who else would leave their cheating husband in California, trek halfway across the country with their four-year-old son, and attempt to start over?" She tried for a carefree chuckle, but her eyes caught his as he moved into the office. The sound stalled in her throat.

She crossed her legs and gave him a pointed stare, but her gaze didn't flicker to his injured leg.

"Sorry I'm late." He settled on the corner of his dad's desk, ignoring Kelly completely though his fingers curled into fists, needing to corner and interrogate the man who'd cheated on her. "What did I miss?"

His father glanced up at Squire. "Miss Kelly said she can get Three Rivers back in the black."

Squire snorted. "How did *Miss Kelly* say she'd do that?" He reached down and opened a drawer in the desk. He pulled out a thick stack of file folders. "Because our last guy left us in a mess of trouble." He dropped the files, which were incomplete financial records, on the desk. They made a deafening bang.

Kelly flinched. She swallowed, a nervous movement that drew his attention to the slender column of her neck. Frustration frothed inside his chest, filling and fighting and overflowing until he felt choked with longing for a future that could never come to fruition. He wished he could go back in time and stop himself from asking her to the prom. Maybe then he'd have his dignity. Maybe then he could look her in the eye. Maybe then he'd be glad she'd applied for this job.

"I'd need to see the files in order to articulate a proper plan," she said, only a slight tremor in her voice.

His dad nudged the stack forward. "Take 'em."

Kelly eyed the paperwork, which probably weighed more than she did. She stood and dragged the folders toward the edge of the desk, staying a healthy distance from Squire. "I can come back tomorrow with a proposal."

"No need," his dad said, and Squire knew what was coming next. He stood up and put his hands in his pockets in an attempt to look bored.

Sure enough, his dad said, "You're our only applicant. If you think you can do this, the job is yours."

Kelly stared at him, unblinking.

A shiver squirreled down Squire's back at the same time his stomach clenched. "Dad, let's not be hasty." He glared at Kelly like she'd somehow bewitched his father into offering her the job. He knew she hadn't, just like he knew it was easier to act like a jerk to put distance between them. If she didn't like him, then she'd avoid him. The very thought made his heart tumble to his shoes, but he needed the distance.

He turned away from her and leaned closer to his father. "We can't afford another disaster."

"I won't let you down," she said.

Squire's blood squirmed in his veins at the assurance in her voice. He couldn't believe her. She'd let him down before and didn't even have the decency to admit it. He gave her another sweeping glare as his father clapped his shoulder.

"Show her to her office, son." He tipped his head her way. "Clark out front will give you the paperwork you need."

"Thank you." Kelly smiled and shook his father's hand, but he pulled her into a hug.

"It's good to see you back in Three Rivers, Miss Kelly."

Squire wished he didn't think so too. The fresh ink on her divorce papers felt like a shield he should wield.

"Thank you, Frank." She turned to Squire, almost like she would shake his hand too. He stepped back, a clear message for her to keep her handshakes to herself.

"This way." He led her down the hall, past his office, and into the last one in the back corner of the trailer. It was where he'd discovered the discrepancies between his father's bank accounts and the quarterly reports.

He'd never been so angry. So frustrated. So helpless. Not even when his tank platoon had been targeted in Kandahar and he'd lost four men in his company, been injured himself, and witnessed the more horrific things that fire did to human flesh. No, this betrayal ran deep, and it meant his parents couldn't afford to retire anytime soon.

Squire had never felt the love of ranching the way his father had, and his father's father before him. The ranch needed to stay in the family if his parents had any chance at surviving financially, which made it disappointing that Squire didn't have an older brother.

But he understood duty, always had. Even though he wanted a different life, somewhere else, if his dad wanted to retire, Squire would do whatever he could to make the transition easier.

Kelly flipped on the light and entered her office. She'd lugged the files with her, and Squire considered taking them from her. *What could it hurt?*

But he knew what it would hurt. He'd worked too hard for too long to build those walls around his heart.

"Let me take those," he said anyway, his voice much softer now that he was alone with her. She had to stretch up while he bent down, his forearm cradling hers, as she transferred the load to him.

She stumbled, her shoulder crashing into his ribcage. A grunt escaped his mouth, and she gasped. "I'm sorry." She stepped back and tugged on the bottom of her jacket.

"It's fine." He moved to the desk, a definite limp in his step and a flush rising through his neck. He watched as she inspected the built-in filing cabinets, ran her finger along the blinds covering the single window, and tested out the chair behind her desk.

She finally looked at him. "I like it."

"Great," he said dryly. "It's not like we'd change it if you didn't."

She gave him a withering look. "Come on. It's me, *Kelly*." She tried a smile, and he allowed himself to return it halfway.

He knew who she was. She was the girl who danced with his sister. Who slept over on the weekends. Who'd bewitched him so completely he'd convinced himself a senior would go to her prom with a sophomore. If she'd gone with someone else, he might've understood.

He shoved the sourness down his throat where it belonged.

While he hadn't been this close to Kelly in years, the real prize she offered was solving the ranch's financial problems. He couldn't forget that.

He'd moved on with his life. So had she. She'd gone to college, gotten married, had a kid. And now a divorce.

He allowed himself to fully smile. Maybe she wasn't out of his league anymore. *She most definitely is*, he corrected himself as he stepped closer to where she sat. "You still know any of your dance moves? Besides that pathetic high kick, of course."

She threw her head back and laughed. "I'm sure I could choreograph something for you. Remember when I used to do that?"

"Yeah. You and Chelsea were so annoying."

"I'm sure we were." The glint in her eye spelled *mischievous*. "So do you make it a habit to leave helpless women trapped in your stairs?"

"You're hardly helpless, darlin'." Squire sat in the chair opposite of her desk with his arms crossed.

She busied herself with the files, shifting them around without really changing anything. "I also don't remember you being such a scoundrel." Though she'd moved away from Three Rivers, her Texas twang remained. He liked it, and wanted to hear her say his name in her pretty little voice.

"I don't remember you wearing such high heels," he shot back.

The silence lengthened between them, until Kelly asked, "How's your mother?"

She hadn't forgotten her Texas manners while she'd been gone. Squire would give her that. "She's good. She's given new definition to the word overbearing now that she knows how to text. But she's good."

Kelly leaned forward, and Squire caught a glimpse of her younger self, the girl he'd crushed on so long ago. "You don't like your mother texting you? Why? It cramps your style while you're out digging ditches?"

Squire could've sworn she was flirting with him, but the idea was ridiculous. She was coming off a messy divorce and had moved in with her parents. He'd heard what she'd said about moving halfway across the country alone. She wasn't looking for a relationship, especially with her new boss.

"As a matter of fact," he said. "It does. Digging ditches requires a lot of concentration. Texting is distracting."

"Don't dig and text." The flirtatious sound of her voice wormed its way straight into his heart. He'd remembered a lot about her, but her voice had faded quickly. He realized now how much he liked listening to her talk. "That is so you."

His pulse galloped, slowing to a trot as he leaned forward, like they might share something meaningful if they got just a little closer to each other.

Her phone chimed, and she jumped up. "That's my alarm. I need to get back." The playfulness and hope drained from her voice and face. She glanced up and smiled, but it had lost its savor. Squire watched the weight of real life descend on her, clouding the girl he'd once known.

"Can you help me get these to my car?" She indicated the folders.

"You don't need to look at them tonight," he said. "You start tomorrow. Look at them then."

She blinked a couple of times, confusion racing through those beautiful eyes. "I'll just take a couple folders." She picked them up and stepped toward the door just as Squire did.

Close enough to feel the gentle heat from her skin, Squire found a flicker of fear in her expression. He wanted to reach out and comfort her, ask her what her ex had done to her to make her so nervous, demand to know how he could have changed her into someone other than the Kelly she'd been.

Instead, he said, "You really don't need to take those. The ranch'll still need your help tomorrow." He moved into the hall ahead of her.

"Is it really that bad?" She joined him, her purse swinging between them.

"Just about." Squire noticed the silence in the front of the trailer. The cowhands had gone out on their assignments for the day, leaving Clark alone at the controller's desk.

"Miss Kelly," Clark said, heavy on the cowboy accent as he handed her a manila folder. "If you fill these out and bring 'em back tomorrow, I'll get y'all on the payroll."

Kelly grinned, tucked the folder into her purse along with the others, and thanked him. Clark barely acknowledged Squire, something he was used to. Clark knew everything about the ranch, from how to run it to how to let it run itself. If Squire was being honest, Clark should've taken over as foreman.

They both knew it, and it seemed like every other cowboy on the ranch did too. He had his work cut out for him to win over the staff and figure out how to manage something as vast as a cattle ranch. He'd tried some of the tactics he'd learned in the Army about taking over a company when the commander had been killed in action. But cowhands weren't soldiers, and they hadn't quite warmed to him the way his comrades in Afghanistan had. Squire had learned that men would trust him when he showed them they could.

He needed to do that at Three Rivers, but he hadn't quite figured out how.

Kelly didn't know any of his failures on the ranch, and she didn't need to. He wouldn't burden her with his unrealized dreams, permanent physical injuries, and financial troubles.

She removed her heels before stepping out of the

admin building, and he had a momentary flash of him sweeping her off her feet and carrying her down the steps.

Longing lashed his internal organs like a whip. Thoughts like that were why he needed to put so much distance between them, why he needed to constantly remind himself of the duties he'd taken upon himself as ranch foreman. He had to find the missing money before he could even think about anything but the ranch.

"See you tomorrow."

Squire focused, the fantasy of him and Kelly dissolving as he realized she'd already made her way down the stairs and to her car. She waved, and he watched her climb into her sedan and drive down the road, kicking up dust as she went.

He frowned at himself, needing a cattle gate on his emotions to keep them contained. He glanced toward the stables, wondering how he could possibly endure day after day with Kelly so close.

Sneak Peek! Second Chance Ranch Chapter Two

Squire went to the house instead of returning to his father's office. He just couldn't muster the energy to learn about fencing issues, the location of aquifers, or the schedule of selling and shipping the herd. He'd helped out on the ranch growing up, but only tending to the horses, riding the fence line, and weeding his mother's massive vegetable garden.

When he'd gotten old enough to learn the business of ranching, he'd gone off to school and then the Army.

He found his mother in the kitchen, bent over a recipe. Squire couldn't name how many times he'd seen her in that exact position. If she wasn't cooking, she was gardening, cleaning, or sewing. He and Chelsea each had at least fifteen quilts to "start them off right" should either of them ever get married.

Thoughts of marriage blasted bitterness through his

bloodstream—because thoughts of marriage conjured never-to-be images of him in a black tux while Kelly clutched his arm and wore a white dress.

"Squire," his mom said, her voice sounding faint and far away. "You okay?"

He blinked his way out of the Kelly-induced fog. "Hmm? Yeah."

"How'd the interview go?"

"Dad hired her." He sat on a barstool to watch his mother cook.

"You're not surprised, are you?"

Peace wafted over him whenever he sat at this counter and spoke with his mom. He smiled at her when she glanced up. "Kelly was the only applicant, and she does have a master's degree in accounting."

His mother pulled open the fridge and retrieved a package of ground beef and two green bell peppers. "You don't sound happy about hiring her."

"She has no experience," Squire said, removing his cowboy hat and running his fingers through his hair. "She might be worse than Hector."

His mother wielded her knife with precision as she split an onion in half. "That would be impossible." She lit the stove and put a cast iron pan over the flame, her gaze sliding over Squire in that assessing way all mothers had. He knew she was looking for something, he just didn't know if she'd found it.

"She's...different," he said, a well of unease pooling where his oxygen should be.

"So are you," she pointed out. "Maybe it will work out this time."

"Mom." Exasperation roared and reared over his previous contentment. "There was no *last* time."

She chopped and diced, drizzled olive oil into the hot skillet, and tossed all the vegetables in. They sizzled and jumped while she added the seasonings. "I know."

Squire didn't think she did. "I'm her boss. I can't go, I don't know, getting involved with my accountant."

"Good point," she said. "You couldn't get involved with your sister's best friend either. But sometimes God has a way of putting people right where they need to be, right when they need to be there." She brandished her wooden spoon at him to enunciate her point.

"Sure, Mom." Squire stood up before she splattered him with sautéed vegetables. He'd gone to church with his parents until he'd left for college. Then Sunday had become the only day to sleep in or get caught up on homework. His faith hadn't dwindled, just his outward manifestation of it.

During his deployments, he'd attended services whenever he could. There was nothing like war to make a man question what he believed. Especially about where he might go after this life. Squire had given a fair amount of thought to the subject, and his belief that God was merciful and kind had been strengthened.

Squire returned to his cabin and changed into his workout clothes. Maybe God could make sure his weight training drove Kelly from his mind completely, though all of his previous pleas to this same end had gone unanswered.

KELLY BURST through the front door of her parent's house, her heart tumbling up her throat. "I got the job!" She dropped her purse as her mom jumped up from the couch in the living room.

"You got the job?"

"I got the job!" She grabbed her mom in a hug, laughing and spinning her around. "I was the only applicant, but I got the job."

The back door slammed and Finn raced through the mudroom and into Kelly's arms. "Mom, guess what?"

"What, baby?"

"Grampa says I threw the ball fifteen yards."

"That's great, Finny." She ruffled his hair, knowing a four-year-old couldn't throw a ball that far. "Guess what? I got a job that will help us get a house of our own." She beamed down at her son, basically a miniature of Taylor. His dark hair; his strong, square face; his unending energy.

Finn's eyes weren't quite as dark as her ex's, but they hovered between green and brown in a beautiful hazel color. The only mark of herself she could see in him.

"I don't want to get a house," Finn said, squirming out of her hug. "Grampa says he's gonna build a new chicken coop, and I can help." He ran through the house to the backyard.

Kelly stood, a sigh escaping her lips. She couldn't live with her parents forever, but having her dad in Finn's life had brought her son's smile back. He rarely left her father's side, and as hammer blows came from the backyard, warmth radiated in Kelly's core.

She moved to the back door and looked through the window. Twenty yards away, out by the shed, her dad bent over several pieces of cut wood, nails clenched in his hand. Finn stood in front of him, a hammer at the ready. She'd never seen Taylor do anything similar with Finn, and as she watched, her mind wandered to Squire. She could definitely see him working and playing with his kids.

"You can stay as long as you need to," her mom said, and Kelly's thoughts about her new boss scattered.

"I know, Mom. But we can't live here forever, even if he wants to." She kicked off her heels and left them by the back door before she moved into the kitchen. "I have a little bit more to go before I pay off the divorce lawyer. Taylor and I agreed to split everything regarding Finn right down the middle. I could probably save enough to put a down payment on a house and move out in a couple of months."

Her mom nodded, tucking a stray strand of Kelly's hair behind her ear. "Where will you go?"

"Somewhere in town." She began to make lunch. Her shift at the grocery store began at two, and while she'd gotten the position at the ranch, she couldn't blow off Vince. She'd give her two-week notice today and hope Vince would let her work on the weekends.

"Maybe over by Crystal," her mom said, watching her set water to boil for the pasta. "There are newer houses on the west side of town."

"Maybe," Kelly said, content as she thought about Finn playing with Crystal's boys. Kelly would like to be close to her cousin too. She thought about taking Finn out to the ranch. The idea of him running free—riding horses, feeding calves, playing in the dirt—made her heart expand by double. Finn would absolutely adore the ranch, the way she had as a child.

And there were a lot of men out there. But Finn just needed one man in his life, someone who loved him and wanted him around. Taylor wouldn't be that man, and again Squire stole into Kelly's mind. She shook him away, stirring her thoughts into the pasta pot until hot water sloshed over the sides.

"Once I have enough saved, I'll look around." Kelly put the wooden spoon down and flashed her mom a smile. Planning more than a day or two out brought a sense of accomplishment Kelly hadn't experienced in months.

Her mom turned the conversation to the weather, a safer topic that gave Kelly some relief from the heavier matters weighing on her mind. It had been an exceptionally dry spring, and her mom worried about the possibility of not having the traditional fireworks show at the upcoming Fourth of July celebration. But Kelly's mind wandered back to the ranch. Nerves crowded her stomach as she thought about going to work tomorrow, of seeing Squire. If only she had a few weeks to review everything she'd learned in five years of college so she could put together a proposal that would impress him.

Finn and her father banged into the house, asking about lunch. Kelly forced away her confusing thoughts about Squire and fearful worries about being inadequate at her new job, painted on a grin, and opened a can of spaghetti sauce.

THE NEXT MORNING, Kelly stirred before the sun rose. Not because of nerves or bad dreams, but because Finn was whimpering. Suddenly wide-awake, she pushed the folders off the edge of the bed where she'd discarded them last night and hurried out of her bedroom. Theirs were the only two bedrooms in the basement, situated right next door to each other, so she arrived at his bedside in seconds.

She stroked Finn's hair off his forehead, and he calmed. "You're feverish. Did Grandpa give you chocolate after dinner?"

Finn moaned, which Kelly took as a yes. She went into the small bathroom in the hall. She had a plethora of children's medications, and she selected one that would bring down Finn's fever quickly. She filled a cup with water and took it in with the pain reliever.

She woke him and made him drink the medicine and a sip of water. He settled right back to sleep, looking angelic in the soft light coming from the bathroom. She carefully lay down beside him on the double-wide bed and closed her eyes. She needed to be up in a couple of hours to get ready for work, but she could hope for a few minutes of rest.

She startled awake at the sound of her mother calling her name. "You'll be late on your first day. Are you ready?"

Adrenaline swamped her, forcing her pulse to drum against her tongue. Kelly took a few seconds to gather her bearings. The spot next to her—in Finn's bed—was empty.

She hustled into her bedroom, but her phone alarm had been silenced. "Finn!" she called as she realized she didn't have time to shower.

"Yeah, Mom?" Finn came bounding into the room, already wearing an adult-sized tool belt held tight by the masterful use of a bungee cord.

"Did you turn off my alarm?" She wasn't surprised at his miraculous recovery. He often ate too many sweets, experienced a low fever and stomach pain in the night, and woke up good as new.

"Yup. You were tired."

"Finn, I have to go to work this morning. Remember

Mommy got a new job?" She flung hangers around in her closet, searching for the right outfit to wear.

Finn watched her, and she finally sent him back upstairs. She couldn't blame him for turning off her alarm. He'd done it many times since they'd moved here.

She sucked in a deep breath. She could only imagine what Squire would say if she showed up late.

She hurriedly stepped into a pair of purple corduroys, matching them with a flowery silk top. She slipped on a more ranch-practical pair of black boots and moved into the bathroom.

A groan escaped as she took in her appearance. She turned on the water and ran wet fingers through her hair to get it to lie down. With a hot cloth, she washed her face. After whipping out the hairdryer and doing a quick fluff, she did a half-decent job on her makeup, and practically sprinted upstairs.

"Breakfast?" her mom asked from the kitchen.

The clock read eight thirty-two. "No time," Kelly panted. "I'll be fine." She kissed Finn, grabbed her purse, and ran out the front door.

She parked next to the ranch trucks at nine o'clock sharp, thanks to some pedal-to-the-metal driving. The shocks on her sedan might never recover, but Kelly would take car repairs over being late.

Squire's dog was already snoozing in the shade as she climbed the stairs and banged her way into the administration building. She glanced around surreptitiously for him, but didn't see Squire in the open area to her left. She handed her folder of paperwork to Clark just as a blond cowboy stood and whistled.

"Well, who is this sweet drink of water?" he asked, swaggering toward her.

Kelly almost laughed out loud, but managed to keep her face placid. Clark answered for her without looking up from her paperwork. "That there's Ethan," he told Kelly. "He's good for almost nothin'."

"I'm good for everything, sweetheart," Ethan corrected as he moved closer. Too close. He smelled halfway between showered and mucking out the horse stalls.

Kelly straightened her shoulders and looked up at him. "Is that so?" She itched to take a step away but held her ground. "Got anyone to vouch for that?"

Ethan settled his arm across her shoulders. "You will be soon, little lady."

"Ethan," a man barked.

Kelly jumped, her hands automatically coming up to cover her spasming heart. Ethan dropped his arm like she'd spontaneously combusted. His second reaction took several seconds longer, but he eventually turned toward Squire.

"Boss." He didn't look ashamed, didn't tip his hat.

Squire steamed like he was four seconds from going into Tasmanian devil mode. His eyes stormed; the muscle in his jaw twitched, and he folded those bulging arms across his chest.

Kelly pressed her lips together to keep her smile contained. She definitely wasn't trying to make sure her lipstick was as fresh as possible.

"Did you get those bulls moved to yard three?" Squire asked.

"Didn't know I was supposed to," Ethan responded.

"I put it on the board for today." Squire hooked his thumb toward a white board behind him in the open area of the trailer where the cowboys had been hanging out yesterday. Kelly only saw two or three there now and assumed the rest were out tending to their assignments.

"Well, then I'll get right on it," Ethan said. "And I'll get back to you later, pretty lady." He tipped his hat to her and with a final glance in Squire's direction, left the trailer.

Kelly noticed Squire's grimace as the door slammed. His teeth clenched and his eyes pressed closed against something only he could see.

"You're all set," Clark said as if he hadn't been present for the showdown that had just taken place. "Here's the password for the computer."

Kelly took the slip of paper and stepped with confidence toward her office. When she reached Squire, she had the strangest urge to reach up and smooth the tension from his shoulders.

"Good morning," she said, focusing on stepping past him without touching him. He smelled like wood smoke and musk, and she silently took the deepest breath she could manage.

"Morning." He followed her through the trailer to her office and sat in the chair across from her desk.

She suppressed her sigh, sat down, and pulled the files from her purse like they could shield her from his presence. "These were pretty messed up." She glanced at him. "What do you know about them?"

"About what you just said. They're messed up." He stared back at her, and again she noticed that he didn't wear normal ranch attire. Today he was wearing jeans, but it was obvious they hadn't spent any time outside in the sun. No belt. Clean, new hiking boots. He wore a short-sleeved button-up shirt in lilac. She didn't think an Army man would be caught dead in purple, but on Squire, the light color served to enhance his muscles.

His cowboy hat sat in place, covering his dark hair, and his striking eyes reminded her that he was dangerous to her health. Everything about him seemed vibrant, while she felt pieced together in yesterday's clothing.

When she realized she was staring, she pulled her attention back to the file. "Why'd you say you didn't recognize me yesterday?" She kept her eyes down. "I mean, you obviously did."

"From what I remember, you like doing things by yourself." His mouth seemed painted in a level line. His arms couldn't clench any tighter across his chest. His tension bled into her, which made her stomach squirm in a wobbly dance.

She flipped open the file, unsure of what he meant by

such a comment. She knew she didn't need him in her office, all up in her business, as she studied their financial records. "I'll let you know when I find something, or when I have a plan for what we should do."

"Great." He stood, reached into his pocket, and extracted his phone. He leaned over her desk to see what papers she had. "I wouldn't start there."

"It was the one on the top," she said, a vein of annoyance working its way into her voice.

"Doesn't mean that's where you should start."

Her stomach chose that moment to emit the loudest growl that had been heard this side of the Mississippi.

He chuckled. "My mother usually serves breakfast at seven," he said. "She might have something leftover. You want me to go get it for you?"

"No," she said quickly. She certainly didn't need Squire bringing her food. She ran her fingers through her limp hair, cringing at the somewhat greasy texture. "I'm fine. I just skipped breakfast this morning. Wasn't feeling well."

He lifted his eyebrows, but not in surprise. More like a challenge.

"Not feeling well?" he repeated. "Nervous?"

"About this job?" She forced a laugh. "No. I've got this. It was something I ate at work last night."

"You have another job?" The eyebrows went down, but she didn't like the compassionate tone in his voice either.

"No," she said. "Well, I do for a couple more weeks. But just on weekends."

"What do you do?"

She really wanted him to leave. Maybe then she could crawl under her desk and bask in the shame of her situation. "I, uh, work at Vince's."

"The grocery store?"

"Don't tell me you've forgotten about them, too." She gave him a look that could melt steel and returned her attention to the files. "Maybe you need to see a specialist about your memory loss." As soon as she said the words, she regretted them. Maybe he'd been injured on one of his deployments. She knew better than anyone that not all wounds were visible.

His low chuckle prompted her to look up, but she refused to give in to the grin tugging against her lips. Her sweet tooth would have to be satisfied with cookies, not Squire's tasty laugh. At the thought of food, her stomach rumbled again.

He flipped through the stack of files and plucked a thick one from the middle. "Start here." He plunked the folder on top of the one she'd been reading, turned, and left her office. She watched him go, noticing that he favored his right leg. Only a slight hiccup in his stride, but present nonetheless.

So he *had* been hurt overseas. Even as she wondered what had happened, relief that he'd left her office flowed through her strong enough to anchor her to why she was there. And it most definitely wasn't to find a cowboy.

———

A wounded Army cowboy, a divorcée with a child, and their second chance to heal old hurts… **SECOND CHANCE RANCH** is available everywhere books are sold! Scan the QR code below to grab it.

Keep reading for a sneak peek at **HER COWBOY BILLIONAIRE BEST FRIEND.**

Sneak Peek! Her Cowboy Billionaire Best Friend
Chapter One

Graham Whittaker gazed at the Tetons, wishing just the tops of the mountains were snow-covered. Unfortunately, it hadn't stopped snowing for a few days, and the white stuff covered everything from the mountain-tops to the grass outside the lodge he'd just bought and moved into over Christmas.

He liked to think heaven was weeping for the loss of his father, the same way the Whittaker family had been for the past nine days. With the funeral and burial two days past now, everyone had gone back to their normal lives—except Graham.

"This is your normal life now," he told himself as he turned away from what some probably considered a picturesque view of the country, the snow, the mountains.

Whiskey Mountain Lodge was a beautiful spot, nestled right up against the mountains on the west and the

Teton National park on the north. It had a dozen guest rooms and boasted all the amenities needed to keep them fed, entertained, and happy for days on end.

Not that it mattered. Graham wasn't planning on running the lodge as the quaint bed and breakfast in the mountains that it had previously been.

No, Whiskey Mountain Lodge was his new home.

His father had left behind an entire business that needed running, and Graham had nothing left for him in Seattle anyway. So he'd come to help his mother after the sudden death of her husband, and he'd had enough time to find somewhere to live and operate Springside Energy Operations as the CEO.

It was a step up, really. He'd only been the lead developer at Qualetics Robotics in Seattle, but the itch to develop technology and robotics to make people's lives easier had died when his father had.

Graham hoped it would come back; Springside could definitely benefit from having the first fracking robot to identify the natural gases under the surface of the Earth *before* they drilled. But they were years away from that.

Just like Graham felt years away from anyone else out here.

A dog barked, reminding him that he'd inherited his father's dog as well as his company, and he went over to the back door to let Bear back in. The big black lab seemed to move quite slowly, though he still wore his usual smile on his face.

"Hey, Bear." He scrubbed the dog to wipe off the snowflakes that had settled on his back. "Guess I better go check on the horses."

Whiskey Mountain had come with a riding stable, something tourists apparently liked to do in the summer months in Wyoming. Graham had grown up in Coral Canyon, Wyoming, but his parents lived in town, in a normal house, without any horses.

Of course, every man in Wyoming learned to ride, and Graham and his three brothers were no exception. But it had been a very, very long time since he'd saddled up in any sense of the word.

But today, though the lodge was a huge building, with dozens of places to which he could escape, he felt trapped. So he plucked his hat from the peg by the door and positioned it on his head. He didn't get many opportunities to wear a cowboy hat in Seattle, but here, he'd worn it every day. And he liked it.

The brim kept the snow off his face as he trudged down the path he'd shoveled every day since moving in and headed toward the stables.

The stables were named DJ Riders, and Graham had no idea where it had come from. There were only three horses that had come with the property, and thankfully, the loft held enough hay to keep them fed for a while.

Graham went through the motions of feeding them, cleaning out their stalls, and making sure they had fresh water that hadn't frozen over. January in Wyoming wasn't for the weak-hearted, that was for sure, horse or human.

The chores done, Graham closed up the stables but turned away from the lodge up the lane. He had plenty of unpacking to do and no inclination to do it. Besides, it would keep, as he'd been living in the lodge for three days without the family pictures, all the dishes, or more than one towel. He'd survived so far, thanks to a four-wheel-drive vehicle and a pocketful of cash.

He wandered away from the stables, the barn, the rest of the outbuildings of the lodge. He passed a gazebo he hadn't even known existed until that very moment, and he wondered what else he'd find on this parcel of land he'd put his name on. And who knew what spring would bring?

Probably pollen and allergies, he thought, still not entirely happy to be back in Coral Canyon though he'd made the decision to leave his job in Seattle and settle back in his hometown.

The snow muted his footsteps and made it difficult to go very far very fast. Didn't matter. He had the whole day to do whatever he wanted. Tomorrow too. It wasn't until Monday that he'd have to put on a suit and start figuring out how to manage an energy company with over two hundred employees.

He approached another building, this one a bit different than the ones he'd seen before. He wasn't sure what it was, though it looked like a small cabin, with a stovepipe sticking out of the shingles on the roof. Did the lodge have a smaller place to live? Was this another guest area he could rent out?

He stepped closer and peered in the window, not seeing a door anywhere. The place was simply furnished and appeared to be one room with a door leading out of it on his right and into what he assumed was a bedroom.

A woman came out of the bedroom, buttoning her coat.

Graham yelped and backed up at the same time a dog put his front paws on the windowsill inside the house and started barking. And barking. And barking.

With his heart pounding and his adrenaline spiking out of control, Graham's brain didn't seem to be working properly. Therefore, he couldn't move. Didn't even think to move.

So he was still standing there like a peeping Tom when the woman lifted the window and said, "What are you doing here?" in a tone of voice that could've frozen the water into snow if the temperature hadn't already done it.

"I—I—" Graham stammered. "Who are you?"

She cocked her hip, and Graham noticed the long, honey-blonde hair as she threw it over her shoulder before folding her arms. She possessed a pretty face, with a sprinkling of freckles across her cheeks and nose. Her eyes could've been any color, as he was looking from the outside in and the light wasn't the same.

If he'd had to, he'd categorize them as dangerous, especially when they flashed lightning at him.

"I am the owner of this property," she said. "And you're trespassing."

Graham frowned, but at least his brain had started operating normally again. It was his pulse that was galloping now, wondering what he had to do to get invited in to find out what color those eyes were.

"Oh," he said. "I'm sorry. I thought this was my place. I just bought Whiskey Mountain Lodge." He waved in the general direction of the lodge, hoping it was the right way.

"The border is back there about a hundred yards," she said, still positioned like he might come at her through the window screen. "There's a fence."

"Maybe it's buried in all the snow." Because he had definitely not crossed a fence line. He might have become a city slicker but he still knew what a fence meant. "I'm Graham Whittaker."

A noise halfway between a squeak and a meow came from her mouth. Those eyes rounded, but he still couldn't tell what color they were. "Graham Whittaker?"

He tilted his head now, studying her. Because she knew him. No one spoke with that much surprise in their voice if they didn't know a person.

"Yes," he said slowly. "I'm...." He didn't know how to finish. Everyone in Coral Canyon knew his father had died. Everyone knew the Whittakers had come to mourn. He supposed everyone though they'd all left again, except for his mother and his youngest brother, Beau, who lived in town and worked as a lawyer.

But he didn't know what he was still doing in Coral Canyon, or why he felt the urge to explain it to this woman.

"Just a second." She slammed the window shut and moved away. Feeling stupid, Graham stood there in the snow, wondering what she was going to do. Half a minute later, the dog that had tried to rip his face off through the glass came bounding through the snow from the front of the house.

"Clearwater," the woman called after him, but the dog was either disobedient or didn't care. The blue heeler came right up to Graham and started sniffing him.

Graham chuckled and scratched the dog behind his ears. "Yeah, I've got a lab. You can probably smell 'im. Bear? His name's Bear."

The blonde woman came around the corner of the cabin, and she stopped much further away than her dog had. "Graham Whittaker." This time she didn't phrase it as a question, and a hint of a smile touched her lips. "You don't remember me, do you?"

Graham abandoned his administrations to the dog and took a step toward her, trying to place her. He thought he'd definitely remember someone as shapely as her, what with those long legs that curved into hips and narrowed to a waist, even in the black jacket she'd buttoned around herself.

He was about to apologize when the answer hit him full in the chest. "Laney Boyd?" He tore his eyes from hers to glance around the land, not that he could tell anything with the piles and piles of snow.

"Is this Echo Ridge Ranch?" he asked. He hadn't realized the lodge property butted up against the ranch where he'd spent time as a teenager. And without looking back at Laney, he knew he'd find a pair of light green eyes. Eyes that came to life when she was atop a horse. Eyes that had always called to him. Eyes that saw more than he'd ever wanted her to. Beautiful, light green eyes he wanted to get to experience again.

When he looked at her again, her grin had filled her whole face. "It's Laney McAllister now," she said, dashing every hope he had of rekindling an old friendship—and maybe making it into something more.

Which is stupid, he told himself as he chuckled and walked through the snow to give her a hug hello. *You just got your heart broken. No need to do it again.*

Sneak Peek! Her Cowboy Billionaire Best Friend Chapter Two

Laney McAllister shook her head as she laughed, the sound more incredulous than happy. She couldn't believe Graham Whittaker had returned to Coral Canyon. Could *not* believe it. The man was twice as broad as he'd been as an eighteen-year-old, his voice twice as deep, his charisma twice as strong.

Her heart leapt and flopped and bounced around as he drew her against his chest and said, "It's so good to see you again." He released her quickly, and she put an extra step of distance between them, the moment suddenly awkward.

"You runnin' the ranch?" he asked.

"Ever since Dad died." And of course, that was why he'd come home too. His father had just passed away, and someone needed to manage the fracking operation that had made the Whittakers one of the wealthiest families in Wyoming.

Pain pinched between his eyes, and Laney wished she could take back her words. She understood the pain of losing a parent so young, and she reached out and put her hand on Graham's forearm. Even through the layers of his coat, a charge passed between them.

It wasn't the first time she'd felt this pulse between them, but it had always been one-sided. Graham had dated the same girl all through high school, and then he'd left for college. Left Emma Darrow here to marry someone else. Left his family to pursue some sort of computer science in the technology hub of the country a few states away. Left Laney, his best friend who'd always encouraged him to do what made him happy.

Now, looking at the strong lines of his face, that cowboy hat that made him rugged and sexy, and those beautiful brown eyes, she could tell he was not happy. Maybe two decades had gone by since they'd truly been in touch—social media and a quick card of condolences when her father had died didn't count—but Laney had known Graham as well as she'd known herself. They'd been best friends for twelve years before they'd graduated and he'd gone to MIT and she'd gone to a university in Cheyenne.

Their lives had taken divergent paths since then, and yet, there he stood. Right in front of her. Looking every bit as vulnerable and handsome and powerful as she remembered.

"I'm sorry about your father." Her voice lifted into the air, barely loud enough for her to hear among the silencing snow and whispering wind.

Graham nodded, his bearded jaw tightening. *The beard's new*, Laney thought. It wasn't very long and the gray that dotted it only reminded her of how many years had passed since she'd seen him last.

"Do you want to come in?" she asked, indicating the cabin. "It's freezing out here." She'd been about to head over to the stables to take care of her horses, but they could wait a few more minutes for their breakfast. And Bailey—

The thought of her daughter hit her like a punch to the chest. Then she remembered that Bailey had spent the night at her mother's and wouldn't be home until late afternoon.

"I think I'll pass." Graham tipped his hat at her. "I don't want your husband to get the wrong idea about us." His dark eyes bored into hers, and the truth bubbled to the back of her throat.

"My husband lives somewhere in the South," she said. "And he's an ex." She cinched her arms across her chest, the emotions that went with her divorce still so close to the surface.

Shock crossed his face. "I'm sorry. I didn't know." A smile touched his lips and as she dropped her hand from his arm, he caught it in his. A squeeze. A nod. That smile.

Oh, boy. That smile did dangerous things to her stomach.

He released her hand half a second before she was going to shake his away. Not that she didn't want to hold his hand. She did. But she didn't need his sympathy. Not over Mike.

"It's been three years. We're managing okay." She took a deep breath—a big mistake what with the sub-arctic temperatures that froze the inside of her nose.

"We?" Though he looked away, back toward his lodge, the curiosity in his voice filled the sky surrounding them.

He'd find out anyway. Coral Canyon was a small town, even if her and Bailey living up at Echo Ridge wasn't new gossip. And Laney wasn't embarrassed about anything anymore.

"Me and my daughter," she said. "Bailey's six."

"Oh." He brought his eyes back to hers. "Where is she now?"

"At my mother's. That's why I was...." She trailed off, the thought of sharing something personal with Graham a little too much to expect at the moment. She'd heard he was back for the funeral, of course. She had no idea he'd been planning to stay.

And while they'd known each other well in high school, that was well, high school. He was thirty-nine now, and she'd be thirty-nine in March.

"Do you come out here a lot when Bailey's gone?" he asked.

"Sometimes," she said. "It's nice to get away." And she rarely had the opportunity to do so. Bailey had a lot of chores, and she did most of them without complaint. But she was still only six and needed constant looking after, as did their four dogs, two cats, and thirteen horses.

"I know what you mean." Graham gazed up through the bare branches of the trees beside the cabin and then flashed her a smile that seemed too tight around the edges. "Want me to walk you back to your place?"

"Oh, I'm fine." She waved away his offer, regretting it as soon as her hand fell back to her side.

"Can I get your number?" he asked.

Their gazes locked, and Laney's heart did a weird pittering pattering pulsing in her chest.

"I've been living in the city for a while," he said with a chuckle. "I'm glad to know you're so close. Would you mind if I called you from time to time if I need help?"

She couldn't imagine a single thing the tall, dark, handsome, and rich Graham couldn't figure out on his own, but she pulled out her phone and said, "What's your number?"

He dictated it to her and she sent him three smiley face emoticons. "Now you have my number." She grinned as his phone chimed and he pulled it from his back pocket. Just watching him tap and swipe with that little smirk on his face got her blood heating.

"Well, I have to get to work," she said. "My horses can't feed themselves."

"It would be nice if they could, wouldn't it?" He laughed, the sound delicious to all of her senses.

"How many horses do you have?" she asked, stepping toward the road that led back to the epicenter of the ranch.

"Just the three," he said. "You?"

"Thirteen." They reached the road in front of the cabin, Clearwater at their heels. She pointed south. "Your place is just up there and around the curve." She faced northeast. "I'm down this way."

He let his gaze linger down the road toward Echo Ridge and then said, "Good to see you again, Laney," before turning south and walking down the road. She watched him for too long, but his long, jean-clad legs with those broad shoulders clothed in black leather...he had grown into positively the most beautiful man she'd ever known.

And he'd been gorgeous as a teenager. It almost didn't seem fair.

Sighing, she turned away and reminded herself that she already had enough to do, dozens of tasks to keep her busy. She didn't need to add a man to the list. Oh, no siree. She did not.

———

Exactly thirty hours had passed before Graham's name brightened her phone screen. She flipped the two hamburgers she was frying for lunch before swiping open the call. She eyed Bailey, sitting at the kitchen counter with a coloring book in front of her as she said, "Hey."

"Hey." Graham sounded like he had a smile on his face. "I'm wondering what you know about dermatitis in horses."

Laney laid a slice of cheese on each hamburger patty. "What makes you think your horses have dermatitis?"

"I looked it up on my phone."

"What does it say to do?"

"I have no idea. There's no treatment. I also don't know how it happened. Can you come take a look at the horses?" He spoke in a tone that didn't really allow her to say no. She wondered if anyone ever told him no, and what he'd do if they did.

As if Laney didn't have enough to do. But she said, "Sure," anyway, and said, "I have to go." She hung up before she could give away too many of her irrational and confusing feelings. They'd kept her awake much too long last night as it was, and she couldn't give them more stage time in her mind during the day too.

"Here you go, Bay," she said, scooping the hamburgers out of the pan. "Time for lunch. Put those away."

The strawberry-blonde child began putting her crayons back in the box. "Is there avocados?"

"Not today." Laney smiled at her daughter and added, "But I have tomatoes and lettuce, and the burgers have cheese on them." She put a bun on Bailey's plate. "Make it how you like it."

Laney pulled out a bag of chips they'd partially eaten last week and set them on the counter too. They'd gone into town for church that morning, but she hadn't seen Graham. His mother was there, as was Beau, but Graham didn't sit with them. She hadn't seen any tire tracks leading from the lodge either, and she wondered if he'd stay holed up at Whiskey Mountain Lodge to work, or if he'd take over his father's office in the small building Springside Energy operated out of.

Why Graham Whittaker took up so much of her brainpower was a mystery to her. Frustrating, too. So she banished him as she put mustard, mayo, and ketchup on her bun, added lettuce and tomato and bit into her burger.

"You're coming out to the barn with me," she reminded Bailey as they finished their lunch. "You've got to check on the cats, remember? And the outdoor dogs. And make sure all the chickens have enough feed and water."

"Okay." Bailey only ate a few bites of her burger but plenty of chips. Laney probably should've argued with her about it, but she didn't have the energy today.

She thought of Mike, of where he might be and what he might be doing. No matter what it was, it wasn't dealing with the bills of a ranch that made marginally more than it needed to run, or his daughter's dietary needs.

"School on Monday," she added, as if Bailey had forgotten from the last time Laney had told her. "Back to real life."

"I like Christmas break," Bailey said, a frown pulling at her eyebrows.

"Me too." She ruffled Bailey's hair and put her plate in the sink. "Get suited up. It's cold out there." She stepped over to the back door and pulled on her own boots, then her coat, hat, and scarf. "I'm going to be checking on the cattle today. Stay in the barn when you're done with your chores, okay?"

Bailey agreed, and Laney helped her with her coat and scarf, making sure her daughter wouldn't get frostbite when they went outside.

She pulled her gloves on last and they stepped into the winter weather. The snow had stopped, and the sky was blue and clear. But the sun shining on the landscape only made things bright, not warm. In fact, it was even colder now that the cloud cover had moved on.

Their breath steamed in front of them as they made the trek across the back lawn and into the barns and stables.

"Cats," Laney reminded Bailey. "Dogs. Chickens."

"Cats, dogs, chickens," Bailey recited back, and she got to work with the two cats she'd named herself. Laney watched her feed KC, short for Kitty Cat, and Meow, the two stray cats Bailey had kept in her bedroom until Laney had smelled them.

With everything else they'd lost, she couldn't make Bailey get rid of them, so they'd compromised. They could be barn cats, catching mice and running around the ranch. But they simply couldn't stay in the house.

Laney only let two of the dogs in as it was, and she glanced over to the outdoor mutts—Georgia and Savannah—on her way toward the back of the barn. She loved her ranching life, she really did. But some days, especially in the dead of winter, she wondered what it would be like to have a husband who went out in the cold and took care of the chores while she stayed inside and sipped tea and baked cookies.

Not that she was the tea-drinking cookie-baking type of woman. But she knew some women who were, and she never felt like she fit in with them. That, combined with living so far out of town, meant most of her conversations happened with Bailey or a bovine. Her gaze wandered to the south as soon as she stepped outside, but she couldn't see even an inkling of the lodge from her property.

It sat up the hill, but then down in a swell, and the only time she even knew it was there was when she drove by to go to town. Still, now that she knew Graham lived there, she could somehow feel his presence.

She worked through feeding the horses, even when her hands felt like they might fall off and they were bright red. By the time she checked all the cattle feeding troughs and took care of the ice, the salt licks, and the thrush that had popped up on a few of her cows, the daylight had begun to fade.

Every bone in Laney's body wanted to go back to the house and snuggle into a blanket with Bailey, hot chocolate warming her from the inside out as a movie played at low volume in front of them.

She found Bailey in the barn, cuddled up with the two dogs and the tablet Laney let her use after she did her chores. "Come on, Bay. I'm finally done."

The girl looked up at her and slowly got to her feet. "Did you know that orangutans' arms stretch out longer than their bodies?" She held her arms out as if she were an airplane. "Humans don't do that."

"I didn't know that," Laney said, smiling at the ground as they picked their way back to the homestead. Once inside, she slipped a pizza in the oven and changed out of her cold and wet clothes.

"Hot chocolate?" she asked her daughter, who had also changed and was now feeding the indoor dogs.

"Yeah, sure." Bailey wandered over to the couch and sat down while Laney zipped around the kitchen to get the mugs, milk, and powder out. With the first mug rotating in the microwave, she remembered Graham and his request to come help with his horses.

A groan pulled through her throat. She could easily text him and say she couldn't come. But part of her wanted to help him. The part that found it funny that he thought he could just show up in backcountry Wyoming and run a lodge and stables when he hadn't come back to Coral

Canyon for much more than holiday dinners over the past two decades.

In the end, she finished the hot chocolate and pulled the pizza out of the oven when the timer went off. Bailey had switched on the TV, and Laney swept a kiss across her daughter's forehead. "I have to go help someone for a few minutes," she said. "Will you be okay here?"

Bailey took a sip of her hot chocolate while guilt pulled strongly through Laney. Although Bailey was only six years old, she could be alone for a half an hour.

"I'll lock the doors, and you've got Clearwater and Barry here," she said. "And the phone Grandma gave you. Call me if you need me. I'll just be up the road a bit."

Bailey nodded and went back to watching TV. Laney pulled her boots back on though her feet protested at the indication that they'd be returning to work.

It's for Graham Whittaker, she thought, hoping her old feet would get the message and just get the job done.

———

This Christmas, can Graham and Laney build a family and find their happily-ever-after? **HER COWBOY BILLIONAIRE BEST FRIEND** is now available everywhere!

Keep reading for a sneak peek at **LAST CHANCE RANCH.**

Sneak Peek! Last Chance Ranch
Chapter One

Scarlett Adams wiped her dirty hands down the front of her jeans, wondering what her life had become. She'd only been at Last Chance Ranch for two weeks, but it felt worlds different than the life she'd left in Los Angeles, only thirty miles away.

That couldn't be right. Thirty miles?

She sighed and scraped her sweaty flyaways off her forehead. Surely this place was at least three universes from the life she'd known on Earth.

This was your choice, she told herself as she surveyed the room holding more stuff than she'd ever owned in her life. Yes, her mother had called her and said her grandfather needed help. And Scarlett had seized the opportunity to leave the city, something she'd been wanting to do since her divorce had become final.

No, she wasn't wearing skirts and silks and heels

anymore. She'd thought those things made her happy, but she knew now that they didn't. Of course, neither did sleeping as late as she wanted, wearing jeans all the time, and cleaning out years of her grandfather's hoard.

So maybe she hadn't thought through this life choice as much as she should have. But how was she to know Gramps hadn't thrown anything away since Grams had died? It wasn't like Scarlett came out to the ranch all that often, despite the short distance from her previous apartment to this sprawling piece of land in the Glendora foothills, right at the base of the Angeles National Forest.

She was still in California—it only felt like she'd blasted off to the moon and was trying to organize it.

She picked up a jar with an unknown substance in it, hoping it was well-sealed and would stay that way. Probably something Grams had canned decades ago. Maybe grape juice. Scarlett wasn't entirely sure, and she wasn't going to find out. She'd rented an industrial-sized dumpster that she filled faster than the sanitation department would come pick it up. She'd made great progress on the ranch, getting the homestead cleaned out, as well as the three spare cabins that sat just behind the main house.

There were thirteen other cabins that sat near the entrance of the ranch, along with that robot mailbox she'd loved as a little girl. She smiled thinking about the contraption her great-grandfather had welded together and which her older brother had dubbed Prime, because he'd been learning about prime numbers in school at the time and there was only one robot mailbox like the one guarding Last Chance Ranch.

Those cabins had been empty for a while, and Scarlett hadn't done much to them to make sure they were habitable. If she wanted to save Last Chance Ranch, she'd need to fill them with men and women willing to work. She'd need to find a way to pay those people. And she'd need to figure out how to get Gramps to let go of some of the stuff he thought he couldn't live without.

Scarlett knew what he was doing wasn't considered living. And she knew that what he couldn't live without he couldn't get back. Grams.

Another sigh left her mouth, and she gently set the jar of whatever-it-was in the wheelbarrow she was using to haul trash from what used to be a sun room to the dumpster. Oh, yes, this would be a sun room again, and she'd sit here with Gramps while he drank black coffee and she sipped chamomile tea. Oh, yes....

She dug back into the work, ignoring the sun as it continued to beat down on her. Item by item piled into the wheelbarrow until she tried to lift it and could barely do so. She hefted it into position and started for the dumpster, which was concealed on the east side of the homestead. That way, when the director for Forever Friends, the animal organization Scarlett had contacted to come see the facilities at the ranch, arrived, she wouldn't see all the trash.

In fact, Scarlett was hoping to get all the trash off the

premises before Jewel Nightingale showed up. Considering that the woman hadn't even responded to one of Scarlett's emails or phone calls kept her resting easy at night.

Oh, and all this physical labor. That certainly had her sleeping like a baby in a way her marketing executive job never had.

She passed a half a dozen cars and trucks on her trek from Gramps's place to the garbage container, and she had no idea what to do about those. Gramps claimed none of them ran, and Scarlett certainly didn't have the skill set to fix them. She could probably sell them and get some much-needed cash for the ranch if she could get any of the engines to turn over.

"At least Gramps has all the keys," she muttered as she approached the trash bin. She couldn't lift the wheelbarrow up and over the lip of the dumpster, so she'd been throwing items in one at a time, or shoveling them in with a strong, plastic snow shovel she'd found in one of the barns.

How Gramps had ever bought a snow shovel in California, Scarlett wasn't sure. But it worked great to get trash up and into the container.

In the distance, dogs barked from their runs in the area of the ranch Scarlett had affectionately called the Canine Club. Gramps loved the dogs too, and he spent most of his time with them on the north side of the ranch. When she'd asked him how many dogs lived on the ranch, he'd said, "Maybe twenty."

"Maybe?" Scarlett hadn't meant to screech the word. "You don't know how many dogs live here?"

"There's at least twenty," he'd said again. And so, when Scarlett's muscles screamed at her to stop using them so strenuously, she'd go out to the different regions of the ranch—Canine Club, Feline Frenzy, Horse Heaven, Piggy Paradise, and LlamaLand—and document what lived there. What breeds, if she could figure it out. How many dogs, cats, llamas, horses.

She'd searched on the Internet and asked Gramps dozens of questions about what the animals ate and how he paid for the food. He seemed to have a schedule of volunteers coming out every day, seven days a week, to walk dogs and play with cats.

Oh, and the ranch had come with exactly one cowboy —a man named Sawyer Smith who gave horseback riding lessons on Saturday mornings, took care of the horses and cattle, and managed the majority of the crops on the ranch.

Scarlett had hardly ever seen Sawyer in the two weeks she'd been at Last Chance Ranch, and that was just fine with her. At forty-three-years-old, she was not interested in another romance. Nope. Not happening.

She finished unloading the last of the trash from the wheelbarrow, the thought of returning to go through more garbage almost so depressing she could fall to her knees.

But she didn't. She kept her back straight and clapped her work gloves together, sending dirt and dust into the air.

The dogs were really barking up a storm.

Scarlett left the wheelbarrow behind as she stepped onto the dirt lane in front of the homestead and started down it. Another road forked to the left a ways up, and that led to Canine Club and several barns where the goats lived.

If she were being honest, goats terrified her, and she'd never been happier to have brought a friend with her to the ranch. Adele Woodruff had worked in the city with Scarlett, and she'd needed a fresh start somewhere with less smog—and less likelihood of a debt collector showing up while she was trying to answer phones. Adele lived in the cabin right next door to Gramps, and she'd been tending to the goats, claiming she had a great way to start bringing in cash for the ranch.

She wouldn't tell Scarlett what it was though, but she worked in the pastures and goat arena for hours with the animals.

Scarlett didn't see her as she passed the cat houses and entered the Canine Club. "What's going on?" she asked Annie, a white bulldog mix who seemed to be the matron of the club. "Where's Gramps?"

She opened the gate and entered the dog community, where she'd documented a whopping twenty-six dogs lived. "Maybe twenty" had been way off, and the budget to feed and care for these dogs exceeded what Gramps brought in from his social security and Grams's death benefit.

Scarlett really needed the partnership of Forever Friends, and she needed it quickly. After deciding she'd call Jewel again once she got back to where she could wash her hands, Scarlett pushed her fear away.

She had a lot of savings, and while she'd lost a lot in the divorce, it wasn't all monetary. She wouldn't allow herself to think of Billy and Bob for more than a moment. A quick whisper of thought, and then gone. It hurt too much that she didn't have her own fur babies with her on this ranch where twenty-six other dogs lived. Billy and Bob would've loved the Canine Club, and they should've been there with her.

"Gramps?" she called, the moment where she thought of her own dogs over.

He didn't answer, but a distinctly male voice said, "Hey, do you own this place?"

Scarlett spun toward the voice to find a tall, dreamy man wearing a cowboy hat and holding a leash.

"Scooby?" she asked, sure this man's name wasn't the cartoon character. "What are you doing with my dog?" Anger and iciness was the only defense she'd have against this man, she could tell.

"He was out on the road," the man said, glancing down at the big brown boxer. "Hound managed to make friends with him while I got the leash on."

Scarlett noticed the golden retriever at the man's side

—no leash required. So he had enough charm to make dogs do things according to his command. Of course he did. Scarlett felt his charisma and charm tingling way down in her toes.

"I wasn't sure if he came from up here or not. I just followed the sound of all the barking."

"He belongs here," Scarlett said, stepping forward to take the leash from him. "Scooby, you've got to stop digging under the fences." And not just because Scarlett struggled to fill in the holes.

"I'm Hudson Flannigan," the man said, reaching up with his now-free hand to lift his cowboy hat and push his hair back. He had dark sideburns and at least three days' worth of a beard to match his salt-and-pepper hair, and Scarlett's heart betrayed her by sending out a couple of extra beats.

He was her age.

So what? she asked herself in a harsh mental voice. She was used to looking for and finding details no one else did, and this man clearly hadn't bathed in a couple of days. Probably as long as it had taken to grow that sexy scruff.

She gave herself a mental shake as she found the tattered cuffs on his jeans, the well-worn cowboy boots, the soft sparkle in his eyes. And the hint of grease under his fingernails.

"I noticed your mailbox on the way in," he said, that voice like melting butter.

"What of it?" she asked, trying to keep a grip on

Scooby, who probably weighed as much as she did. She almost scoffed out loud. That so wasn't true. She was no lightweight, and though she'd lost ten pounds since coming to the ranch and starting the physical labor, she was easily still a size fourteen.

"It looked like it could use a tune-up," he said. "Some of the pieces need to be welded together again."

She narrowed her eyes at him. "And I suppose you're just the man to do it." Did he wander the foothills, looking for jobs?

"I could," he said. "I'm a master welder and I'm not bad with horses either." His dog laid down, his tongue out like this was the most boring conversation on the planet.

An idea formed in Scarlett's mind. She definitely needed help with the horses. She'd been tending to them every morning and evening, but she had no idea what she was doing. "We have sixteen horses here at the ranch," she said. "I have a guy who does riding lessons on the weekend."

Hudson nodded and touched the brim of his hat as if to say, *Point taken. You don't need me.*

"I can't pay you much," Scarlett said quickly. "But I have a clean cabin you can live in. Hound too. And you can fix that mailbox, work with Sawyer in Horse Heaven, and...." She cocked her head, sure she was right about him. "How handy are you with cars?"

Sneak Peek! Last Chance Ranch
Chapter Two

If Hudson Flannigan had been doubting why he'd turned up this obscure road when he'd heard a dog bark, he quit the moment that auburn-haired beauty asked him how handy he was with cars.

"I do all right," he said evasively. He didn't need to go showing his whole hand at once. He also couldn't help the steady prayer that started in his head and wouldn't stop.

Please, please, Lord. I need this job. Please help me get this job.

Over and over the words looped through his mind. Of course, if God cared all that much about Hudson, his marriage of ten years wouldn't have fallen apart. Or at least the Lord would've given him a clue that his wife was being unfaithful. Or maybe the fact that Hudson had lived so long in unknowing bliss had been more merciful of the Lord. The jury was still out on that one.

And Hudson had been down and out since the divorce, almost a year ago now. He hadn't stayed in one place longer than a couple of months, and the constant travel was tiring.

The woman nodded toward his hands. "Looks like you've worked on one recently."

"Just my truck," he said, wanting to hide his hands.

"Well, I'm Scarlett Adams, and I'm running this ranch with my grandfather. He's got at least six vehicles on the property that need fixing, and if you do it, I'll split the profit with you."

Hudson's eyebrows went up. "What kind of split?"

"Eighty-twenty," she said without missing a beat.

He scoffed, almost offended but enjoying this game with Scarlett too much. "You're joking, right?"

"We own the vehicles. They just don't run."

"Which makes them useless," he said. "I'll go...eighty-twenty in my favor."

She gaped at him, those beautiful eyes like pools of pond water he could dive into and swim around in. When she started laughing, Hudson smiled.

"You're a funny guy," she said, still giggling and still holding onto that boxer like she was trying to choke him.

Hudson stepped forward and took the leash from her. He let it slacken and hang at his side, saying, "Stay, Scooby." The dog stayed. "I'll just help you get him back inside then," he said. "I didn't own and operate my own mechanic shop for twenty years to fix someone else's cars and not get paid for it."

He moved past her, hoping she'd counteroffer. A place to live out on this beautiful land sounded mighty appealing.

Please, he thought again, wishing the last time he'd been to church wasn't a month ago. But surely God understood why Hudson hadn't gone. It was hard when people asked where he lived and he couldn't give them an address.

He tried opening the door to the building she'd been standing in front of, but it was locked. Just like last time he'd tried. Maybe this gorgeous woman had distracted him too much.

"It takes a key card," she said, squeezing in beside him and swiping a card in front of the reader. The door clicked, and she gestured for him to go in.

He did, his head swimming with the strawberry scent of her hair. She was dirty too, and somehow that added to her allure. "Where do you want him?"

"Over here." She stepped over to one of the empty pens in the circular room. With ease, she pulled the bolt up and the gate swung in.

Hudson unclipped Hound's leash from around the other dog's neck and said, "Go on." Scooby moved into the pen, and Scarlett locked him inside before facing Hudson again.

"Fifty-fifty," she said.

"I want to see the cars," he said.

Her eyes blazed with fire that wasn't entirely angry, but that he knew would burn him just the same. And he didn't mind. In fact, he thought he might like to be torched by this woman.

No, you don't want that, he told himself. He'd been operating on half a heart since Jan's betrayal. He hadn't been able to go home, as his mom loved Jan as much as him. In fact, since the divorce, she'd hosted a birthday party for his ex-wife and they still played Bunko together monthly.

Hudson had always been a disappointment to his horse-training father, who didn't understand how any son of his could be content with being a mechanic. So Hudson had wandered from San Diego to Sacramento, looking for odd jobs, anything that would fill the tank in his truck and get him something to eat.

Another day. Another dollar. Another job.

"Fine," Scarlett clipped out. "Come with me."

"C'mon, Hound," he said as he followed the curvy woman back outside. The view was certainly better than any he'd had in a while, and he found another smile forming on his face.

His pulse seemed to start with the pleadings, every beat pushing out a *please-please. Help-me. Please-Lord.*

Scarlett marched down the road, Hudson matching her stride for stride. "There's a couple of trucks," she said. "Four cars, and that's all in the main yard. There's tractors and stuff in the equipment shed, though Sawyer says those run okay."

"And do they?" he asked.

"I don't really know," she said. "I think everything around here needs a lot of attention and a good cleaning, the vehicles included." She shot him a look out of the corner of her eye that he wasn't sure if it was a glare or just a glance. "I've only been here for two weeks, and Gramps...well, Gramps is eighty-one-years-old, and a hoarder."

Compassion ran through Hudson. She was stepping into a situation she couldn't control. And making the best of it. Hudson had some experience with that, and he knew what kind of grit and determined spirit a person had to possess to do it.

"There they are," she said, going around the corner of the house and stopping.

He paused too and took in the row of vehicles in front of him. The trucks were old—older than him, and maybe as old as her grandpa. If he could get those running, they'd fetch a lot of money.

The cars seemed to be old sedans, nothing important or all that note-worthy. But if they ran, and the upholstery was in good shape, he could get a few thousand for them. People bought cars like that for their teenagers all the time.

The numbers added up in his head, and he'd take fifty percent if she'd give it to him. He said, "Those cars aren't worth anything. The trucks, maybe. Seventy-thirty."

"Sixty-forty."

"For me?"

"For you."

Hudson peered at the row of vehicles like he was really thinking about it. Several long moments passed, and then he said, "Deal."

She turned toward him, that long dark red hair swinging in its ponytail. "Deal." She extended her hand and he took it, ignoring the fizz of attraction now simmering in his bloodstream.

They shook hands, and she said, "I'll get the paperwork drawn up. Do you want to see the cabin?"

———

AN HOUR LATER, Hudson filled Hound's bowl with fresh, cold water from the hose on the side of his new cabin. He left the dog to drink as he went up the back steps and into the cabin Scarlett had let him choose for himself.

There were thirteen almost identical cabins here at Last Chance Ranch, and he'd chosen the one in the corner of the U-shaped arrangement. It had a bigger yard for Hound, and a row of huge oak trees along the grass that would shade his place from the setting Western sun.

"Thank you," he whispered to the empty room, the kitchen on his right, dining room on his left, and living room in front of him. The cabin was a box, with a hallway that led to a bedroom and a bathroom on the other side of the kitchen. So not somewhere he'd live and raise a family, but for him and Hound, it was perfect.

Absolutely perfect.

It had running water, which meant he could shower every day. A washing machine and dryer took up space in the bathroom, which meant he could wash his clothes whenever he wanted. There was a single couch in the living room, a table with two chairs in the dining room, and a bed, so he didn't have to live in the back of his truck with the camper shell anymore.

His was full-size, and he could stand up almost all the way right in the doorway. If he wasn't so tall, he'd be fine. His bed sat at the back of the truck bed, and he passed a kitchen with a microwave, sink, and two-burner stove on his left to get to the bed. He had plenty of storage for his stuff, and a bench he could sit on to put on his boots. But no toilet. The shower had a twenty-gallon tank that stayed hot when he decided to use it. He also had a built-in heater and air conditioner in the shell. Not that he needed the temperature regulators in May in California. He had used the heater a few times on rainy days in the winter, especially farther north.

He'd been eating a lot of microwaveable meals and canned foods, already prepared things like granola bars and bags of chips, and as he gazed at the full-sized stove and oven in the kitchen of this cabin, he thought he'd died and gone to heaven.

He could cook. He could do laundry. He could bathe.

Hudson had never been happier, and he bent to retrieve his backpack so he could get out his charger, plug in his phone, and get it powered up while he showered. Then he'd call his brother Brent and tell him all about the stray dog that had provided him the opportunity to be proud of himself again.

After all, in the course of the last couple of hours, he'd gotten a job. A place to live that wasn't on wheels. And a pretty redhead who kept popping up in his mind's eye, despite her frosty reception of him.

He frowned into the warm spray of the shower—his best bath in months, by the way. He wasn't looking for another girlfriend. His heart and life had been through the shredder lately, and he just needed something stable to figure out how to be the new Hudson now that he wasn't part of a couple.

The past year had been one of great learning for him, but it was mostly how to be by himself. He wasn't sure who he was without Jan, or how to be that person in a permanent place. It was easier to be a good person and be kind when he was just passing through.

Now, though, he'd have to figure out how to be kind and good and Christ-like when he saw the same people day after day.

Refreshed from his shower, he went out to his truck and got his welding tools together, determined to get his first job on this ranch complete. When he opened the front door, he found Scarlett coming up the steps with an older gentleman on her arm.

With her eyes down, she didn't see him immediately, so he said, "Hey, let me help." He moved to help her grandfather up the steps, and the old man looked up with pale blue, watery eyes.

"Gramps wanted to meet you," Scarlett said. "He said Scooby is his favorite dog, and he's just so grateful you found him and brought him back." Her voice carried a measure of sarcasm and she rolled her eyes halfway when Hudson looked at her.

"Oh, it was no problem," Hudson said, his kindest voice employed. He smiled at Scarlett and then her grandpa. "I'm just glad I found where he belonged." He looped his hand through the old man's arm too and steadied him as he moved up the steps.

"Gramps, this is Hudson Flannigan. He's going to fix up all the vehicles on the ranch." She beamed at her grandfather and then Hudson, the brightness of her smile fading a bit when their eyes locked.

But for Hudson, his whole soul lit up like a solar flare, and he had a hard time tearing his eyes from hers.

"Good, good," her grandfather said. "That lawn mower stopped working a few weeks ago, too. Maybe he could look at that."

"I could," Hudson said as a feeling that he'd just signed on for a heck of a lot more than he'd thought. This ranch needed a lot of work—it was called Last Chance

Ranch, after all. And Hudson definitely felt like he was on his last chance.

Can Scarlett and Hudson find the faith and forgiveness they need to fix themselves as they restore Last Chance Ranch to its former glory? Find out in **LAST CHANCE RANCH**! Scan the QR code on the next page to find it from your favorite shop!

Tripp (Book 2): She needs a husband to keep her son. He's wanted to take their relationship to the next level, but she's always pushing him away. Will their trivial tie take them all the way to happily-ever-after?

Liam (Book 3): She's desperate to save her ranch. He wants to help her any way he can. Will their invented I-Do open doors that have previously been closed and lead to a happily-ever-after for both of them?

Jeremiah (Book 4): He wants to prove to his brothers that he's not broken. She just wants him. Will a fake marriage heal him or push her further away?

Wyatt (Book 5): To get her inheritance, she needs a husband. He's wanted to fly with her for ages. Can their pretend pledge turn into something real?

Skyler (Book 6): She needs a new last name to stay in school. He's willing to help a fellow student. Can this wanna-be wife show the playboy that some things should be taken seriously?

Micah (Book 7): They were just actors auditioning for a play. The marriage was just for the audition — until a clerical error results in a legal marriage. Can these two ex-lovers negotiate this new ground between them and achieve new roles in each other's lives?

Gideon (Book 8): It's 1971, and Gideon Walker is on the cutting edge of all the technology coming out of Texas. He has big dreams and wants to make something of himself. Then he meets Penny Aarons, and everything changes. He only has eyes for her, but she's got plans and dreams of her own...

Read this origin romance for Momma and Daddy from the Seven Sons series today!

Three Rivers Ranch Romance™ Series

Escape to Three Rivers, Texas for small-town charm, sweet and sexy cowboys, and faith and family centered romance. You'll get second chance romance, friends to lovers. older brother's best friend, military romance, secret babies, and more! The Three Rivers cowboys and the women who rope their hearts are waiting for you, so start reading today!

Second Chance Ranch (Book 1): After his deployment, injured and discharged Major Squire Ackerman returns to Three Rivers Ranch, wanting to forgive Kelly for ignoring him a decade ago. He'd like to provide the stable life she needs, but with old wounds opening and a ranch on the brink of financial collapse, it will take patience and faith to make their second chance possible.

Shiloh Ridge Ranch in Three Rivers Romance™

Meet the cowboy billionaires in the southern hills outside of Three Rivers! They love God, horses, the land, and family, and all 12 of them are looking for love in the small Texas town where they grew up. Start this Christian family saga romance series and spend time with people you'd be happy to call YOUR family too!

The Mechanics of Mistletoe (Book 1): He can be a teddy or a grizzly. She's a genius with a wrench. Can the pretty mechanic tame this cowboy's wild side, or will they both be left broken-hearted this Christmas?

Second Generation in Three Rivers Romance™

Step back into the heartwarming small Texas town of Three Rivers! Get ready to experience a small-town saga like no other, where the legacy of the past meets the promise of the future. As you journey through these heartwarming stories, you'll not only fall in love with the next generation of cowboys and ranchers but also have the joy of revisiting beloved characters from Three Rivers Ranch, Seven Sons Ranch, and Shiloh Ridge Ranch!

The Cowboy Who Came Home (Book 1): He's been serving in the military for a decade. She's been quietly grieving a devastating loss. When Finn and Edith reunite in small-town Three Rivers where they grew up together, can their second chance romance provide hope, healing, and the happily-ever-after they both crave?

About Liz

Liz Isaacson writes inspirational romance, usually set in Texas, or Wyoming, or anywhere else horses and cowboys exist. She lives in Utah, where she writes full-time, takes her two dogs to the park everyday, and eats a lot of veggies while writing. Find her on her website, along with all of her pen names, at authorelanajohnson.com